★ American Girl®

TENNEY
A Song for the Season

by Kellen Hertz

Scholastic Inc.

Published by Scholastic Inc., *Publishers since 1920.* SCHOLASTIC and associated logos are trademarks and/or registered trademarks of Scholastic Inc. The publisher does not have any control over and does not assume any responsibility for author or third-party websites or their content.

Cover design by Angela Jun
Author photo credit, p. 175: Sonya Sones

americangirl.com/service

ISBN 978-1-338-13703-3

10 9 8 7 6 5 4 3 2 1   17 18 19 20 21

Printed in China 62 • First printing 2017

For Mikayla, Kaiya, Owen, and Kieran

CONTENTS

HITTING A HIGH NOTE

Chapter 1

I closed my eyes and replayed the memory once more: bright lights, our music filling the auditorium, my foot stomping on the Ryman stage to the beat of Logan's drums, a crowd of cheering fans. The last hour had been one of the most important times of my life, and I wanted to remember every detail forever.

A gust of air swirled around me, sending chills rippling down my spine. My eyes flashed open. Music throbbed from the stage as people hustled around in the wings, carrying instruments, coils of wire, and sound equipment. Another burst of cold air made me shiver and I hugged myself. The silver spangled concert dress that my little sister, Aubrey, had picked out for me was beautiful, but it wasn't exactly insulated. I edged forward and peeked around the curtain. The golden sea of the Ryman Auditorium stage shimmered before me, filled with musicians playing shining instruments. From where I stood in the shadows, it was like staring into the sun. In a heartbeat, I forgot I'd ever been cold.

Had I really just been playing on that very same stage? Had we *really* just opened for the last show of Belle Starr's world tour?

Just then Belle herself sashayed into view, her platinum blonde hair glowing under the stage lights. She twirled around her two backup guitarists, holding a cordless microphone covered in glittering rhinestones.

"This is the time when dreams come true . . ." she sang.

Fans waved their arms to the beat of the music as they sang along. It was easy to see why Belle was one of the biggest stars in music right now. It wasn't just her clear, bright voice. It was the way people connected to her music. I couldn't help but wonder: *Would my songs ever make people feel that way?*

Someone nudged my shoulder. My bandmate, Logan Everett, stepped beside me. Sometimes it's impossible to figure out what Logan's feeling, but as he watched the show, his eyes were round with awe.

"This is so incredible," he whispered to me. "I still can't believe we're really here."

"I know," I whispered back.

Logan and I had been performing as a duo for less than a year. Our families and manager had always warned us how hard it would be to break out in the music industry, and so we worked extra hard to prove ourselves. It hadn't always been easy, but eventually we became a good team.

So when Belle Starr asked us to open for her final tour show at the Ryman, it felt like we'd woken up in some kind of fairy tale. Logan and I practiced our set for months, fine-tuning every chord transition and harmony until each song felt airtight. And now we knew that our hard work had paid off—we had just performed our best show *ever*.

We'd started out shaky from nerves, but our mistakes were small enough that I figured nobody would really notice. Halfway through our set, I glanced offstage and saw our manager, Zane Cale, in the wings, grinning as he tapped his orange cowboy boots to the beat. I could tell he was proud of how far we had come. But the craziest moment was when I spotted Belle Starr herself watching our show from the wings and singing along to our song "Someone Who Believes"! That's when I *knew* that I would remember this show forever.

Onstage, the music swelled as Belle and her band reached the final chorus of her hit song "Star Like Me." It was Aubrey's favorite song, and I had heard it about a million times. But right now, I felt like Belle was singing directly to me and Logan:

> *You can be a star like me*
> *Know who you are and you'll be free*
> *Be proud of yourself and love what you see*
> *That's when you'll see who you can be!*

Belle bounced up to the edge of the stage. As she hit the song's final high note, she leaped into the air. The song ended with a crash of drums, swirling rainbow lights, and an explosion of colorful glitter fluttering down to the stage. The roar of the crowd thundered through the theater, like a rolling wave.

HITTING A HIGH NOTE

"Wow," Logan breathed, wide-eyed.

I nodded. When we had ended our set, the crowd cheered enthusiastically. But Belle had just taken her fans from enthusiastic to wild.

The applause continued even after Belle loped offstage, waving and blowing kisses to the crowd. The moment she crossed into the shadows of the wings, she kicked off her high heels and wiped sweat from her forehead. She looked tired—until she spotted us and perked up. Before she could say anything, though, a flock of assistants crowded around her. A stagehand swapped Belle's sparkly microphone for an open bottle of water as her hair-dresser fixed some loose strands of hair and a makeup artist waited with a huge powder puff. Belle drank half the water bottle in one gulp and gave us a smile.

"Hey, what did you think of the show?" she called to us from behind a cloud of face powder.

"It was awesome!" Logan and I blurted in unison.

"Jinx," he whispered, elbowing me.

"Glad you liked it." Belle laughed. "That was

some opening set you guys played! You really pumped up the audience!"

I blushed and was surprised to see color rise in Logan's cheeks, too, as he self-consciously ruffled his sandy-brown hair.

"What are you doing for an encore?" he asked.

"I was thinking we could play 'Reach the Sky,'" Belle replied.

My breath caught in my throat. "'Reach the Sky'?" I repeated.

"Yeah," Belle said with a wry smile. "You know that one?"

I nodded so fast I felt like a bobblehead. *Of course* I knew "Reach the Sky." It was one of *my* songs. Belle Starr wanted to perform a song that I had written!

"I'm not sure I'll be able to remember all of the words, though," Belle said, her eyes twinkling. "Do you think you guys could perform the encore *with* me?"

My jaw dropped open, and Belle laughed.

"Don't look so shocked," she said, giving me an affectionate nudge with her elbow and grinning at Logan. "You guys rocked your opening set. The crowd would love to see you onstage again! What do you say? Do you want to help me out with some harmonies?"

Logan and I didn't even have to consult.

"Yes!" we both said at once.

"Great!" Belle said with a merry laugh. She swung her acoustic guitar's strap over her head, slipped on her high heels once again, and winked at us. "Let's go!"

Assistants swooped in, plugging in our earpieces and handing us our guitars. When we followed Belle back onstage, the crowd screamed so loudly I could hardly think straight. We stepped up to the microphones at the front of the stage. The lights seemed hotter than they had before. I wiped a bead of sweat from my hairline and took a deep breath. I had been nervous when Logan and I had performed our set, but now we were playing with the biggest superstar in Nashville. I knew I couldn't mess this up.

"Please give a warm round of applause for my friends, Tenney and Logan," Belle said into her microphone. The audience responded with whoops and whistles. Belle continued with a grin. "As a special treat tonight, we're going to play for you a song written by our very own Miss Tenney Grant. This one's called 'Reach the Sky.'"

Belle's hands danced across her guitar frets, her fingers picking out an intricate accompaniment. I tapped my hand against my leg to keep time. Then we sang, our three voices blending, and I closed my eyes. When I opened them, dozens of tiny flashes of light were exploding across the wide velvety darkness before us as fans took photos. It was like looking into a sky of shooting stars. I never wanted it to end.

SUPER AMAZING

Chapter 2

Once the concert was over and the audience had poured out of the building, there was an after-party set up in the Ryman's lobby to celebrate the end of Belle's tour. Logan and I changed out of our show outfits and met outside our dressing rooms to make our way to the lobby. As we wandered through the maze of cement hallways, I began to wonder if we were lost. Just then, I heard the click of high heels behind us.

"Hey!" Belle said, catching up to us. She wrapped her arms around Logan's and my shoulders and squeezed us in. "Thanks for helping me end my tour the right way, you two!"

"There's a right way?" cracked Logan, raising an eyebrow.

"Absolutely!" Belle said merrily. "Personally, I've

always had this crazy superstition about tours that the first show and last show are the most important."

"Why?" I asked.

"Well, the first show sets the tone for the rest of the tour," she explained. "But the last show is the one you'll remember forever. And y'all sure made it memorable!"

"Are you sad that the tour's over?" Logan asked.

"Gosh, no!" Belle said with a little joyful skip. "I'm thrilled!"

"Really?" I said. The idea of touring the world and playing music every night seemed like the ultimate dream come true. I couldn't imagine why anyone could want that to end.

"Don't get me wrong," Belle said like she'd read my mind. "I *love* performing. But touring's really tough."

How could traveling all over the world and playing shows for sold-out crowds be tough? I thought. But before I could ask, the doors to the lobby swung open and a crowd of well-wishers swept Belle off in a wave of congratulations.

Logan and I stood in the doorway scanning the

crowd for people we knew. Belle's musicians and
touring crew mingled with VIPs, friends, and family
in front of the ornate staircase leading to the balcony.
Finally, we spotted my parents talking to Logan's
mom near the buffet.

"Such a great show, you two!" Mom said.

Dad clapped Logan on the back and pulled me
in for a hug. "Your encore with Belle was fantastic!"
he exulted.

"It was," Mrs. Everett said, kissing Logan on the
head. "I wish your father could have seen it. He
would be so proud!"

Sadness flickered across Logan's face, and I knew
that he was missing his dad. Mr. Everett was a
backup guitarist for a band that had been on tour in
Asia for what seemed like forever.

"Hey," I said to Logan, pointing to the buffet
table of food and drinks behind him. "You want to go
grab a snack? I haven't had anything to eat or drink
since before we got to the Ryman!"

Logan nodded gratefully and followed me over
to the buffet. I grabbed a can of fizzy water and a
plate, piling it high with fruit, a pair of cheesecake

bites, and a trio of chocolate chip cookies. Logan loaded up on so many desserts that it looked like his plate might collapse under the weight. He stuffed an entire cookie into his mouth.

"Whoa, slow down there," I said, laughing.

"I'm hungry!" he replied, spraying crumbs everywhere. "I feel like I just ran a marathon."

I nodded. "Me, too. But it *was* a great show, wasn't it?"

"Sure was," Logan said. "Though we were a little off at the top of 'Music in Me.'"

"I know," I agreed. "I stepped on your cue, sorry. But only because *you* started in too fast!" I said, poking Logan's arm playfully.

His plate wobbled, sending a brownie bite to the floor. "Man down!" he cried.

As he crouched to pick it up, I noticed that Zane had joined our parents, and was speaking to them with wild gestures.

"Wonder what that's about," I said, just as Zane spotted Logan and me and waved us over.

As we slipped through the crowd to them, I could see Zane was holding out his phone, showing our parents something. The moment we reached them, Zane turned to us, his eyes crackling with excitement.

"Great news!" he exclaimed, looking from me to Logan. "A bunch of audience members recorded your encore with Belle tonight. They posted it online and her fans are loving it! It's already trending!"

"Really?" Logan said.

Before Zane could reply, his phone started buzzing and dinging as if it was having a dance party. "More new e-mails," he said, glancing at the screen. As he read, he let out a low whistle and pushed his hat back on his head with a grin. "This one's from a booker I know in Chattanooga. He's got an event next month that he thinks you two would be perfect for . . . Which brings me to my next big idea: We need to think about going on tour."

"R-Really?" I stammered in surprise. "Me and Logan . . . on tour?"

"Yes, ma'am," Zane said with a chuckle.

My heart did a joyful flip-flop, but when I glanced over, my parents were already exchanging concerned looks with Logan's mom.

Seeing their expressions, Zane grew serious. "We need to watch how the online enthusiasm for Tenney and Logan evolves and then sit down and talk about how to build on that," Zane said. His phone dinged again, and he looked around at our parents. "At the rate that this video is spreading, I'm thinking we'll want to get them on the road before the year ends."

"But it's already November," Dad said.

"Which is why we need to start making decisions as soon as possible," Zane urged. "Is there a time y'all can come down to the office to discuss it?"

The adults all started comparing schedules, but I didn't hear any of that. I was looking at Logan. His eyes were wide with the kind of overwhelmed exhilaration I was feeling, too. *A tour!* It's what every musician dreams about, and Zane was considering it as a possibility for us!

The whole drive home, my insides were fizzy with excitement.

"Do you know how incredible it would be to go on tour?!" I told my parents, bouncing nonstop in my seat. "It would be amazing! No, *beyond* amazing. Über amazing. SUPER amazing!"

SUPER AMAZING

"You seem . . . interested," Dad said with a chuckle.

"You guys *have* to let me go," I begged.

"Tenney, we don't even know if it's a real possibility yet," Mom said gently. "A tour is a big deal. There are a lot of moving parts, especially with the holidays coming up next month. I don't want you missing school or getting overwhelmed."

"I promise I won't! I'll work so hard; I won't miss any homework assignments," I said, my brain racing. "If Zane can make it work so I don't miss school, will you let me go?"

My parents exchanged a glance for what seemed like a crazy-long time.

"Probably," Mom finally said.

I squealed again, even louder. I couldn't help it!

Some things are worth losing control over, I thought to myself. And my first real tour was definitely one of them.

ALL IN THE DETAILS

Chapter 3

" *A* re you serious? An actual *professional* tour?" my friend Holliday asked, her eyes sparkling. "That's amazing!"

It was the morning after Belle's concert, and as soon as I'd arrived at school I found my best friends to share the news about Logan's and my maybe-tour.

"Congratulations!" Jaya bubbled, giving me a squeeze.

"Well, we're just talking about it, nothing's official yet," I told them. I didn't want to make a huge deal about it, but just the fact that Zane had brought up touring as a possibility felt like a victory, and I'd wanted to share the excitement with my close friends.

"Will you have tour posters and T-shirts?" Jaya asked as we headed to class.

"And a tour bus like Belle Starr's?" Holliday

ALL IN THE DETAILS

added. "I heard she has a full kitchen and a bathtub *in* the bus. Imagine driving around the country in a fancy tour bus with TENNEY & LOGAN painted on the side! Staying at luxury hotels! Playing at the biggest venues!"

"Guys, nothing's been decided yet," I reminded them, though I had to admit it all sounded *really* exciting.

But Holliday and Jaya didn't seem to hear me. As we arrived at our classroom door, they were still chattering about how glamorous the tour was going to be.

As I sat down at my desk, I pictured everything that Holliday had described. Riding around in a sparkling tour bus, playing for sold-out crowds of screaming fans, jumping around on a fancy hotel bed twice the size of my bed at home.

It all seemed too good to be true, and suddenly I was nervous. What if Zane couldn't make our tour happen? Or what if my parents decided that I couldn't go? And how long would I have to wait to find out whether my wildest dreams were about to come true?

TENNEY

As it turns out, I only had to wait a couple of days. After school on Wednesday, my parents drove me to the Mockingbird Records office on Music Row to meet with Zane.

Ellie Cale, Zane's niece, met us in the lobby. Ellie was the talent scout for Mockingbird, and had "discovered" me while I was practicing a song at Dad's instrument shop last year.

"Your encore with Belle sure is making a splash online," Ellie said to me as she guided us to Zane's office.

I smiled bashfully, but I was too nervous to think of a smart response.

Logan and his mom were already sitting on the leather couches in Zane's office when we walked in with Ellie. Logan glanced at me, his knee bouncing a mile a minute. I could tell he was just as nervous as I was.

Once my parents and I had taken our seats, Zane cut right to the chase. "Belle's fans posted about a dozen videos," he started, looking down at his notes.

ALL IN THE DETAILS

"Each one has been viewed about twenty thousand times by now, and the number of hits you're getting has been *increasing* every day, not decreasing."

"Whoa," Logan whispered.

"Videos of Tenney and Logan's opening set are also getting a lot of online views," Ellie added. "As a result, we've had a healthy stream of inquiries from people wanting to know more about you. Some of them even want to talk about booking shows."

I looked at my parents. Their faces were calm. I took that as a good sign.

Zane turned to Logan and me and continued. "Since your show at the Ryman, I've had a couple of phone calls with your parents, and we all agree that we want y'all to be able to build on the enthusiasm for your music that is brewing online."

"Definitely," said Mrs. Everett. My parents nodded.

"Okay, so what does that mean?" I asked, afraid to say my hope out loud and then have it not come true.

"What it means," Zane said, "is that you two are going on tour."

★ ★

TENNEY

On tour! I wanted to jump up and down and do cartwheels around the room. Instead, I let out the kind of squeal I haven't made since I was five.

Logan clamped a hand over his ear and laughed.

"Sorry," I said, trying to compose myself.

"That's okay," he said, still smiling. "I'm excited, too. Maybe just warn me the next time you're going to make a noise like that so I can get out some earplugs."

Zane grinned. "There's just one catch," he continued. "We need to get this show on the road ASAP to maximize the momentum y'all have right now."

"Absolutely," Ellie agreed. "With the holidays coming up, people are looking to book musicians for holiday fairs, music series, even parties."

Logan perked up. "Wait, so we're going right *now*?" he asked.

"Wh-what about school?" I stammered, my brain spinning. "I have a math test on Monday, and a field trip next week and—"

Mom laughed and put her hand on my knee. "Believe me, honey, there's no chance we're going to let you two traipse off and miss a month of school!" she said reassuringly.

ALL IN THE DETAILS

"Oh," I said, feeling relieved and sort of disappointed at the same time.

"So when *is* the tour going to start?" Logan asked curiously.

"In about six weeks," Zane replied. "That will give me time to line up all the tour dates, plan our travel, and get your album ready."

My breath caught in my throat. Logan quickly covered his ears in case I squealed again, but he looked just as excited as I was.

"Our first tour *and* our first album?" I whispered, as if saying it any louder would make it untrue. I had dreamed of recording an album since I started writing songs, and now it was really happening.

"When do we start recording?" Logan asked, as if he was reading my mind.

"Unfortunately, we don't have time to record a new album from scratch," Zane explained. "I've been recording your live shows ever since you signed to Mockingbird, and I'm going to patch a few songs together to make an EP to sell on your tour."

Logan and I shared a dubious look.

"But what performances are you going to

include?" I asked. "If I'd known that we were recording an album during those shows, I would've sung
better." My mind spun as I remembered that one time
when I had a cold and hit a bad note during
"Someone Who Believes," or that day I got distracted
and missed my cue while playing "The Nerve."

Logan nodded. "And I would have added some
really cool drum riffs and—"

"Don't you two worry about that," Zane interrupted. "I promise I will find your best performances,
including your encore with Belle last weekend."

That made me feel a little better. But I still
couldn't help feeling like we were missing a huge
opportunity to record the best album ever.

"Look," Zane said, reading the disappointment
on our faces, "this is just an EP—an extended play
with a few tracks—not a full album. If we sell enough
copies and your tour is a success, then we can talk
about putting together some new songs for a full-
length album."

My heart skipped a beat. I almost squealed
again, but I held my breath instead.

"Alrighty," Zane said, clapping his hands in

ALL IN THE DETAILS

satisfaction. "So can we get back to discussing the tour now?"

I nodded, and Logan's knee started bouncing again.

Zane proceeded to explain his plans for the tour. "You'll begin performing the day after school lets out for winter break. Tenney's dad and I will be with you the whole tour. We'll book between five and seven shows around Tennessee, so we'll be on the road a little less than a week."

"Does that mean we'll miss Christmas?" Logan cut in, slipping his mom a worried look.

"Nope," Zane said. "We'll have you home on Christmas Eve."

Logan sat back in his chair, looking relieved.

"Just as long as you *get* home," Mrs. Everett replied.

"Of course," Zane assured her, cracking a grin. "Personally, my momma would disown me if I wasn't home for Christmas supper."

I took a deep breath, trying to process all of this information. *So much for traveling to far-flung cities across the country,* I thought. There was only so much we could fit into a week-long tour—which was a *lot* less than the month I'd imagined. *Being away for the week before Christmas means that I'll miss a lot of my favorite holiday traditions*, I realized. *Gift shopping with Jaya, the Howl-iday Ramble with my big brother, Mason, caroling with Aubrey . . . At least Dad will be with me the whole time and we'll be home in time for Christmas—*

Mom touched my arm. "Tenney, are you okay?"

I snapped back to attention. "Yes! I'm super excited!"

So what I'll miss out on some of that stuff, I told myself. Christmas happens every year—but my first tour was once in a lifetime!

"Wonderful," Zane said. He leaned forward, studying Logan and me. "For this tour to be a success, we're all going to need to make sacrifices and work hard," he told us. "But I promise, if we do it right, it will take your band to the next level professionally."

When I looked at Logan, I could tell he was thinking the same thing I was.

"That's exactly what we want," I told Zane. Logan nodded.

★ ★

ALL IN THE DETAILS

"Good," Zane said, settling back in his seat. "So for the next few weeks, while Ellie and I book shows and work out logistics with your parents, you two need to do your part," he continued. "I want you rehearsing every day, putting together a tight set of holiday classics mixed with your own songs. I thought you could work with Portia on that."

"Great!" Logan and I said at the same time.

Over the past year, Portia Burns had become a mentor to me and an unofficial coach for our band, helping Logan and me learn how to write songs together and work out our musical differences. Logan and I both trusted her.

"Okay, then," Zane said. He stood up and walked around his desk, clapping Logan and me on the back. "Congratulations, you two. You're going on your first tour!"

Everyone started talking at once as Zane and Ellie shook my parents' hands and Mrs. Everett hugged Logan. I took a deep breath and imagined myself playing a big holiday show with Logan, both of us singing our hearts out in the crisp winter air before a crowd of screaming fans. Then I dared to picture myself in the recording studio, headphones clamped over my ears as Logan and I sang a duet into huge microphones for our first *real* album.

Sure, I'll miss out on some holiday fun, I thought. *But if this tour is a success, it'll make my greatest dream come true.*

A TIME OF GIVING

Chapter 4

By the first Saturday in December, Logan and I had put together a solid set and were meeting with Portia three times a week to rehearse, rehearse, rehearse.

The sun was shining that morning, but I still had to turn up my jacket collar as I walked from Dad's instrument shop to Portia's house. The wind had an icy edge, like the world was trying to remind me that winter was finally here. Fall and winter in Nashville can be unpredictable. One minute there could be a warm streak, the next it's snowing. You never really know what's around the corner. Still, today was cold, no question about it. By the time I got to Portia's house, the chill had blown pink into my cheeks and my ears were numb.

I climbed the short stack of steps to the front

door decorated with a wreath of orange-gold maple leaves. Portia answered my knock almost immediately. She had on a violet-colored sweater, and her gray hair was braided and looped around her head like a crown.

"Why, if it isn't Miss Tennyson Evangeline Grant," she said, pronouncing my full name with relish and a wry wink.

She led me inside to the sitting room, where Logan was already planted on the couch with his guitar. We said our hellos and fell into the routine of our rehearsal warm-up.

As Portia made tea and Logan started playing scales, I snapped open my case and lifted out my aquamarine guitar. I pulled the strap over my head and began tuning. I listened to each string in turn, my eyes roaming the room. It was as cozy as it had always been, stuffed full with furniture, instruments, and memorabilia from Portia's decades of performing. But now I noticed that Portia had added some holiday decorations. Strings of lights edged the wide picture window, and above the fireplace, red velvet ribbons and fresh green mistletoe hung over an

antique mirror. Along the mantel, boughs of fresh
pine had been placed between framed photos of
Portia's friends and family.

"Christmas is my favorite time of year," I said
with a sigh.

Portia set a tray of tea and cookies on the coffee
table and smiled. Logan must not have heard me as
he focused on his guitar scales.

"On Christmas morning we have a big breakfast
and then take turns opening presents," I continued.
"And after that we always have a family holiday jam,
where we sit around in our pajamas and play music
together all day."

"That sounds pretty cozy," Portia admitted. She
turned to Logan. "What's your family doing for the
holidays this year?"

Logan silenced his guitar and gazed at the steam
rising from the teacups. "I dunno," he said, his mouth
tightening into a sad knot.

I studied his face, remembering how much
Logan had been missing his father. Was he thinking
of him now?

"Will your dad come home this year?" I asked.

"Probably not," Logan said, an edge forming in his voice. "It's really expensive to fly from Asia."

Suddenly, I felt bad going on about all the fun things my family does for the holidays when Logan wasn't even going to get to hug his dad on Christmas.

"I'm sorry," I said.

Logan's cheeks turned bright pink, like he was self-conscious, but he shrugged. "Everyone always says the holidays are full of joy," he muttered. "But nobody ever talks about how they can make you sad."

Portia was watching Logan carefully, too. "Here's what I think," she said. "Sure, the holidays can be lonely. But this season is also a time of giving. It's an opportunity to remind people how much we care about them."

I nodded, waiting for Logan to reply, but he just shrugged and kept his eyes locked on his guitar.

"We should get started," Portia said after a moment. As she moved to grab her guitar, I sat by Logan on the couch.

"Are you okay?" I whispered.

"I'm fine," he replied, but his voice wobbled.

A TIME OF GIVING

Sympathy swept through me. I wanted to say something to make him feel better, but I wasn't sure what that would be. Instead, I made a silent promise: This holiday season, I would find a way to show Logan that I cared.

That afternoon, Mom rounded up our whole family to "holiday up the house," our family tradition of putting up the tree and the indoor and outdoor decorations. It was always a ton of work but it was fun, too, and I'd been so busy rehearsing with Logan for our tour lately that I was looking forward to it more than ever.

Once Aubrey and I had hauled every box of decorations into the living room, Mom put on a Patsy Cline holiday album, and the three of us sang along as we worked. Our golden retriever, Waylon, joined in, too, howling as we hit a high note.

Through the window over the couch, I could see Dad and Mason outside on the porch, wrapping tiny lights along the railing, their breath freezing in the air as they chatted. Dad laughed and clapped Mason on the back. When Dad spotted me watching them, he grinned and started playing air guitar. Mason joined in, playing "air drums" until the three of us cracked up. I turned back to the warm glow of the living room, cozy happiness like a blanket around me. *This is what I look forward to every holiday season*, I realized. *Being with my family like this.*

"I can't wait until the holiday jam," I called to my mom over the music.

Mom smiled. "I have a feeling that this year will be our best holiday jam ever," she said. She hung an heirloom velvet banner reading JOYFUL MUSIC over the fireplace and stepped back to make sure it was centered.

"Mom and I are going to sing a duet!" Aubrey said, reaching into a box and pulling out a set of bottle-brush evergreens.

For a fleeting moment, my stomach sank. Usually, my mom and I performed a duet at the jam, but I had been so busy with tour rehearsals that we hadn't had time to prepare anything. Anything. *Most likely, I won't have time to learn a new song for the jam*

A TIME OF GIVING

this year, I realized. Then I reminded myself that I was happy for Aubrey.

"Your first jam duet!" I exclaimed. "That's so exciting!"

Aubrey grinned. "The only thing that could make our duet better is a concertina," she declared. "I really, *really* hope that Santa will bring me one this year."

"You've mentioned that," Mom said.

"Like, every day for the past six months," I added.

"That's because concertinas are so tiny and cute, and they sound so pretty," Aubrey crooned. "Plus, all the best musicians play *two* instruments, and I only play the accordion. That's why I *need* a concertina."

"Instead of being focused on what you *need*," Mom said gently, "why not focus on what you're going to do for others?"

I perked up, suddenly remembering what Portia had told Logan and me: *This season is also a time of giving. It's an opportunity to remind people how much we care about them.* With only a few weeks left before the tour,

I realized I didn't have long to find the perfect gift for Logan.

"Hey, Mom, do you think we'll have time to go Christmas shopping before I go on tour?" I asked.

"We can try, honey," Mom said, "but you've been so busy with rehearsals and homework that you've hardly had time to join us at the dinner table."

"I know," I said. "But it's really important to me to find the perfect gift for Logan."

"Honey, true generosity isn't always about finding someone a 'perfect' gift," she said. "And remember, the best gifts don't always cost money."

I knew she was right. But what would that look like?

When it came to Logan, I often felt, well, discombobulated is a good way to put it. When we performed onstage together, our music flowed as if we shared a heartbeat. But when he got moody or withdrew from the world, I didn't know how to reach him. I needed to find a gift that would show him that I am his true friend—onstage *and* behind the scenes.

READY TO GO

Chapter 5

The next few weeks passed in a whirl of school, rehearsals, and meetings about the tour. I was so busy that sometimes I had to remind myself to stop and take a breath. Whenever I thought I'd have enough free time to think about Logan's Christmas gift, I was too exhausted by the end of the day even to shop online. Maybe I would find the perfect gift while we were on the road, I decided.

When my alarm went off the morning of the first day of our tour, I was already awake. I shot out of bed, took a shower, got dressed, and lugged my suitcase downstairs. My parents were already up making eggs, toast, and sausages in the kitchen.

"Ready to go, I see?" Dad cracked, rumpling my hair. "Zane's not picking us up for another half an hour. Besides, we need something hearty before we hit the road."

I slumped against the wall and groaned. "I want the tour to start already so I won't have to think about it anymore and I can just enjoy it!"

My parents laughed.

It wasn't long before Aubrey bounced downstairs and Mason slouched into the kitchen from his room. Once breakfast was ready, we all sat down together for one last family meal before the tour began.

"Are you super excited?" Aubrey asked me.

"Of course!" I said, scooping a big forkful of scrambled eggs into my mouth.

"You should be," Mason said. "It's going to be awesome! Even Waylon agrees. Right, Waylon?"

Our dog was curled up in a furry golden circle under a patch of sunlight streaming through the sliding patio door. At the sound of his name, he did one of those happy sleep twitches, showing his belly.

"He's probably dreaming about the Howl-iday Ramble," Mom said.

READY TO GO

I grinned. The Ramble was a yearly neighborhood parade where everyone dressed their pets in holiday-themed costumes and walked them around the park. Last year I had dressed Waylon in a doggy top hat and an ascot, like Ebenezer Scrooge.

"Don't worry, Waylon!" Aubrey said, jumping out of her seat to scratch his belly. "This year we're going to have the best time ever. I'm going to walk you all by myself."

"And I'll keep you company," Mason said. "Although I'm sure Waylon will miss Dad and Tenney."

A pang of sadness hit me as I watched Aubrey cuddle Waylon. Mason and I had gone to the Howliday Ramble together every year since we adopted Waylon as a puppy. It was strange to think I wouldn't be there this time. I shrugged, shaking off the momentary melancholy that was starting to settle. *I can walk Waylon next year*, I thought, just as I heard wheels coming down the driveway.

I ran to the kitchen window and looked out. In front of our garage, Zane was hopping out of a big white van with "Mockingbird Records" emblazoned on the side.

That's no tour bus, I thought. But I had to laugh at myself. It was silly to have assumed that I would be riding in a big fancy tour bus—after all, I was no Belle Starr . . . not yet at least!

I ran back to the kitchen. "Zane's here!" I announced. I swallowed my last bite of toast and put my plate in the dishwasher. Then I yanked on my coat and ran outside.

Zane already had the van's back doors open. Inside I could see microphones, cables, and an amp, all of which I knew were from Mockingbird's studios. There was also a big cardboard box of CDs. *Our EP!*

"Hey there, showstopper!" Zane greeted me. "You ready to get on the road?"

Part of me wanted to jump up and down squealing "Yes!" but I also wanted to look professional, so I just nodded. I took one of the EPs out of the box. Our band name, Tenney & Logan, was splashed across the front of the case in bright bold letters.

"Can I keep one?" I asked.

"Of course," Zane said with a smile. "You and

Logan can take a few for your families, but we need to sell the rest. I'm hoping that we can sell around a hundred fifty of these. Then we can start talking about recording a full album."

I did the math in my head. That meant we had to sell just thirty CDs at every show. *Easy peasy lemon squeezy,* as Mom liked to say.

By the time Dad brought out my guitar and our suitcases, our whole family had gathered by the van. It took only a minute to load everything. Then it was time to say good-bye.

"Keep the calls and texts coming," Mom told us.

"And photos!" Mason echoed. "We want to feel like we're on tour, too."

"You got it," Dad said, hugging him.

Mom turned to me, her gaze calm and strong.

"Even though I'm not going, I'll still be with you," she said.

"I know," I whispered, wrapping my arms around her.

Then Aubrey hugged me, talking the whole time. "If you have questions about how to accessorize, let me know," she told me seriously. Aubrey had helped me pack my suitcase the night before and *insisted* that I bring every necklace, pair of earrings, and hat that I own.

Mason rolled his eyes. "Don't worry about how you look, Tenney," he told me. "Just make sure you rock every show to the fullest. Make people know they need to listen to you."

"I will," I promised, the passion in his words stirring me up.

We finished our good-byes and got in the van. As Zane backed down the drive, Mom, Mason, and Aubrey waved until the van pulled around and drove us out of view.

Our next stop was Logan's house, which was just a few minutes away. When we pulled up, he was on the front porch with his mom and little brother, Jude, surrounded by stacks of drum cases and his guitar.

"I hope all this can fit in the van," Mrs. Everett said as we walked up.

"Don't worry," my dad said. "We'll get it all in."

"Yep, and you'll get to help unload it!" Zane told Logan with a chuckle.

READY TO GO

"Wait, we have to set up our own gear?" Logan said, looking confused.

"You bet!" Zane said lightly.

Logan's shoulders slumped. "When Belle went on tour, she brought a crew to set up and tear down for each show."

Zane raised an eyebrow, nodding. "Well, Mockingbird's a small record label and so it's a bare-bones tour," he explained. "Some places will have people who can help us set up."

Logan looked disappointed. Clearly the tour he'd been imagining had roadies.

"It'll be okay," I said, trying to stay upbeat.

We all pitched in loading Logan's drum gear and guitar as he hugged his family. Mrs. Everett wiped away a tear, but kept smiling. Jude, on the other hand, was having a harder time saying good-bye. He wrapped his arms around Logan and wouldn't let go.

"Why can't I come with you?" he asked Logan in a pleading voice.

"Because I need you to stay here and help Mom

decorate the Christmas tree," Logan said, keeping his voice light.

"But I want to do that with *you*," Jude said softly, and started sobbing into Logan's chest.

Logan and Mrs. Everett exchanged a look.

"I know," Logan said, hugging Jude tightly. "But I *have* to go. I promise I'll call every day and send pictures, okay?"

Jude nodded, his lower lip trembling. He threw himself onto Logan again.

"I'll be home in no time at all," Logan told him.

Mrs. Everett gathered Jude in her arms, and they walked toward the house as we piled into the van. Logan gazed out the window and waved, smiling as big as he could.

"Can we go?" he said through gritted teeth, still smiling and waving at Jude. Zane started the engine.

As soon as we were on the road, the smile faded from Logan's face. "How long till we get to perform?" he asked.

"Franklin's just over a half hour away," Dad replied.

READY TO GO

"And you'll be onstage soon after that," Zane added. "Once your set is over, we'll get right back on the road and head to Kingsport, where you'll perform tomorrow."

"Good," said Logan, checking the time on his phone impatiently.

"I'm excited to get started, too," I said to Logan. "This tour's going to be great."

"Yeah," Logan said, but something in his voice told me that he wasn't convinced.

SETTING THE TONE

Chapter 6

*B*efore we knew it, we were driving through Franklin's cobblestone-paved downtown with its quaint, picture-perfect shops. I'd been there many times before with my family, and I was excited to kick off our first show there. Main Street had been roped off from traffic, so we drove down a street parallel to it. As we did, I caught glimpses of white-tented craft and food stalls thronging with people. Every building was decorated for the holidays and bustling with shoppers. It was already crowded, even though the festival had just begun.

"This is a huge music day for the festival," Zane said. "A lot of bands are playing today."

"But only one of them is kicking off their first-ever tour," Dad said, winking at me. I smiled, but my stomach did a nervous flutter.

SETTING THE TONE

Zane parked on a side street. "The main stage is just around the corner," he told us. "We don't need Logan's drums for this one—they've got a kit there. Just bring your guitars."

He turned off the van, and we all hopped out. Logan and I grabbed our instruments from the back, and together the four of us tromped down the cobblestones to where the side street opened onto the festival route. The crowd was thick here. Most people were watching the festival stage, where a four-piece Irish folk band was blasting through a brash jig version of "Hark the Herald Angels Sing."

"Follow me!" Zane shouted over his shoulder. As we edged through the crowd toward the band, he led us around the side of the stage to a roped-off entrance patrolled by a security guard. Zane flashed a badge at the guard, who opened the rope and let us in.

The backstage area was a giant tent full of musicians tuning up, winding down, and chatting. Zane found the stage manager, who consulted her clipboard and confirmed that we'd be onstage in about thirty minutes.

"Just enough time to get nervous," Zane said, grinning at me and Logan.

Behind us, the crowd cheered as the Irish band closed their song with a final flourish. My stomach flip-flopped and I turned to Logan, who seemed to have perked up a bit now that we were finally here.

"Do you want to warm up?" I asked.

"Sure," he said, offering a crooked smile that showed me that he was starting to feel nervous, too.

We played scales and vocalized, keeping our coats on as we walked around each other in the nippy air. Then we went over each song in our set quickly, playing the most difficult transitions and discussing introductions. We'd been rehearsing a ton, so we were on the same page about nearly everything.

We'd just finished running through "Cold Creek Christmas," a holiday song of Portia's that still played on the radio every once in a while, when I heard a voice behind me say, "That song sure sounds familiar."

Behind us stood Portia herself, wrapped in a tasseled wool cape, her cheeks red as apples.

"Portia! What are you doing here?" I peeped.

SETTING THE TONE

"Just thought I'd come see my favorite duo kick off their first tour," she said with a warm laugh.

"I'm so glad you're here," I said, hugging her. As I did I realized how tense I'd become since we arrived, and tried to relax.

"So? How are you two feeling?" Portia asked after she'd hugged Logan. "Are you ready?"

"Yes," Logan and I said at the same time.

"Okay, then," Portia said with a throaty laugh.

Zane came over to greet Portia and told us we were on in five.

"Have fun up there," Portia told us. "That's what it's all about."

"We will!" I said, flashing her a smile, but as I followed Zane, Dad, and Logan to the steps leading up to the stage, anxiety prickled through me again. I remembered what Belle had told me after our encore: *The first show sets the tone for the rest of the tour . . .*

That makes this show the most important *one of our tour,* I thought. *We have to nail this.*

There was a huge round of applause as the band ahead of us finished. They exited the stage in a sweaty bunch, shaking hands and congratulating each other. Finally, background music started, signaling a transition time to the crowd.

Zane and Dad went onstage along with two audio technicians. They worked quickly, adjusting microphones and checking cables. Finally, Zane came offstage.

"You should be all set," he told us. "Good luck up there. And don't forget to mention that you have EPs for sale!"

The stage manager stepped onstage. The background music stopped, and the crowd fell silent. "It is my pleasure to introduce two of the youngest and most talented musicians to ever grace the Franklin Music Fest stage," she said. "Please welcome: Tenney Grant and Logan Everett!"

Logan and I gave each other a quick fist bump and climbed the steps onto the stage. The minute I saw the crowd, my anxious prickles crackled into fizzy pops of excitement. *This is it!* I thought to myself. *Our first show of our first tour.* I practically skipped over to my spot center stage. I switched on my two microphones, one for my guitar and the other for my vocals. I looked at Logan behind the drums, and he gave me a thumbs-up.

"Happy holidays, y'all!" I said to the crowd, who cheered in response. "We are Tenney and Logan!" I said.

"Or Logan and Tenney," Logan added from his place next to me. It was a joke we'd done before, and we knew that it always worked to warm up the audience. Sure enough, the crowd laughed.

As I laughed along, I noticed my breath turn to steam in the cold. *Funny*, I thought. *I don't feel cold at all.*

"We're excited to be here!" I said. "For our first song, we'd like to do a classic that y'all may have heard."

Logan nodded. "Feel free to sing along," he added.

We counted off, then started in, our guitar lines weaving together into the complex arrangement that started our version of "Cold Creek Christmas." I stepped toward my microphone, taking a deep breath. Just as I was about to sing, however, an ear-shattering *ZINGGGG!* sounded through the speakers.

I stepped back, stunned, silencing my guitar. "Sorry," I tried to say into the microphone, but it *ZINNNNGED!* again, even louder this time. Some people in the audience put their hands over their ears. Logan flipped off his microphones quickly, and I followed.

"Give it a second, then switch them on again," Logan whispered.

I nodded, composing myself, then switched on the mics again.

"Sorry about that," I said into my microphone. But it was dead. No one could hear me. I strummed a few chords on my guitar, but that mic was out, too.

Panic flooded through me. Audio problems are every performer's worst nightmare—the slightest problem can *ruin* a show. You can't play without amplification. Well, you *can*, but the audience won't be able to hear you. Whenever I've had audio problems, which isn't often, I usually end up waiting awkwardly onstage, feeling gigantically uncomfortable while audio techs try to figure out what's wrong. I did *not* want that to happen here.

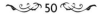

SETTING THE TONE

Stay calm, I told myself, as I switched the microphones on and off again. Still nothing.

"HELLO?" Logan said into his microphone. But his voice sounded like a whisper. Logan stood up from behind his drums, shooting me a frustrated look.

I glanced offstage, but no one was there. I felt frozen, rooted to the ground as wave after wave of anxiety hit me. I had no idea what to do next. Leave the stage? Keep playing even though no one could hear us? I didn't know, so I just stood there, growing colder by the second, as the first concert of our first real tour turned into a total disaster.

THE SOUND OF SILENCE

Chapter 7

J looked out from the stage. Franklin's Main Street stretched in front of me, teeming with festival-goers and holiday shoppers who should have been clapping and singing along to our music. Instead, they were staring at us in quiet confusion.

"Sorry!" I shouted to them. "We're having some audio issues!"

Before I could say anything else, Zane rushed onstage with the two audio technicians from the festival.

"Hang tight, y'all," he told Logan and me. "We're going to fix this ASAP."

"Okay," I said, but I was brimming with worry. Who knew how long this was going to take? We were sure to lose our audience if we didn't play soon.

THE SOUND OF SILENCE

As Zane and the techs clustered around the cables leading to the amplifier at the front of the stage, I edged over to Logan. "What do you think we should do?" I whispered.

"Wait, I guess," he said, but he sounded uncertain.

I sized up the crowd again. Around the edges, people were starting to drift away. Within a few minutes, we would lose our audience entirely.

"Let's play," I said to Logan, and before he could say anything, I launched back into the beginning of "Cold Creek Christmas," playing fast and loud. Logan looked surprised, but he grabbed his guitar and started playing along.

"The lake's iced over and the birds have flown," I belted as strongly as I could. Logan's voice joined mine, blending and doubling our sound in strength.

"The fire's gone out and I'm chilled to the bone," we continued. *"All that's left is my hope that you'll come on home, and share this Cold Creek Christmas with me."*

In the far back, people were still walking off, but the audience members in front of the stage quieted listening to the music. As we sang, both of us instinctively moved toward the front of the stage, belting as loudly as we could. The crowd seemed to move closer to us, too.

They're listening, I thought, my heart spinning in a pinwheel of joy. I started on the chorus.

"May your season sing with joy—"
ZIIIINNNNNGGGGG!

Earsplitting feedback screamed through the stage amplifiers again, stunning Logan and me into silence. The crowd groaned.

Before Logan and I could do anything else, the amps *ZINGED!* again. Zane hurried over to us.

"A cable's gone bad somewhere," he told us. "You guys need to stop playing until they figure out where it is."

"But we're not even using the microphones!" I protested.

Zane shook his head. "We need to get the audio working again," he insisted. "If the audience tries to listen to music right now, they'll just end up frustrated every time we get feedback."

"He's right," Logan admitted reluctantly.

THE SOUND OF SILENCE

I wanted to protest again, but I knew I had to respect Zane.

"We'll be back soon!" I shouted to the crowd, and then shifted my guitar over my shoulder and followed Logan off the stage.

As Zane and the technicians worked on the sound, I watched the crowd from backstage. With each passing minute, our audience grew thinner. It was painful to watch. Finally, after what seemed like forever, Zane came off the stage. He beckoned to us, but as we approached, the stage manager stepped up and started talking to him.

"Is the sound fixed?" Dad asked Zane as we reached him.

"Yes, but there's another problem," he responded, frowning.

"What?" I asked. The festival manager looked apologetically at Logan and me.

"You two were supposed to be onstage for thirty minutes," she explained, "but more than half of that time is gone now. And I'm afraid we can't push the bands after you because our schedule's extremely tight."

"So, what does that mean?" Logan said.

"You can play for only fifteen minutes," she replied.

My heart sank, and the pity in the festival manager's eyes didn't help.

"I'm very sorry," she told us. "It's our only option. Otherwise you can't play at all."

"Okay," I said, gritting my teeth in frustration. "Then I guess we should get going."

Everyone nodded. Logan and I hustled back onstage with our guitars.

"We only have time for a few songs," I told Logan as we moved to our microphones. "Let's start with something they can sing along to."

"How about 'Winter Wonderland'?" he suggested, and I nodded.

I flipped on my microphone.

"Hey, y'all, we're back!" I said as brightly as I could, looking out at the crowd.

Main Street was still buzzing with shoppers, but hardly anyone was paying attention to us. Portia and a few others near the front of the stage were the only people waiting for us to perform.

THE SOUND OF SILENCE

We launched into "Winter Wonderland," as energetically as we could. We sounded okay—at least I *think* we sounded okay. Although I was performing on the outside, inside I was scrambling to figure out what song we should do next. But as the audience grew and a few people started singing along, I started to relax. By the end of the song, I'd figured out what we'd play next.

I turned to Logan and whispered, "'Carolina Highway.'" It was a song my dad wrote. It's rollicking and catchy, so I knew it would get the crowd's attention. Logan must have, too, because he nodded.

We dove into the song, attacking each note. Our pace was fast, and it got faster as people started dancing in front of the stage. After a few measures I started to feel like my head was spinning. When a verse ended, I glanced over to where Dad and Zane stood offstage. They both gestured to me to slow down. I tried, but as the tempo relaxed, the music sounded weird, so I picked it up again. By the last verse, it felt like I was hanging on to a galloping horse. We ended the song with a crash of Logan's drums, and I was glad to see that the audience had finally swelled to the size it had been when we first got onstage.

I took a big breath, relieved that we had saved the show, whatever was left of it. *Now one of our songs,* I told myself. Shifting my guitar in my hands, I started strumming the intro to "The Nerve," a duet that Logan and I had written together.

After a couple measures of the guitar intro, I realized I was playing solo. I glanced at Logan, who was quickly pulling his guitar over his head. He joined in and stepped up to the second microphone at the front of the stage. He leaned over to me. "You forgot to tell me what song was next," he muttered under his breath.

"Sorry," I groaned, feeling my cheeks burn with embarrassment. I started into the song, singing the first verse and letting Logan sing the second. The audience listened attentively and cheered loudly when we finished.

I looked over to Zane, who signaled that it was time to get offstage.

"Thank you," I said into the microphone.

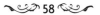

THE SOUND OF SILENCE

Then I heard a voice ring out from the crowd. "Play 'Reach the Sky'!" a young girl shouted.

I looked to Logan, who shrugged, and then to Zane again. The stage manager was standing next to him, waving us offstage and tapping her watch. Zane shook his head apologetically.

I squinted into the audience and saw a girl around my age looking at me with hope in her eyes.

"Sorry," I mouthed to her. She looked disappointed.

I quickly leaned into the microphone again. "Don't forget we have records for sale and—" Before I could say more, my microphone switched off and background music started playing on the speakers.

Zane gave me and Logan brisk shoulder pats as we came off the stairs into the backstage area.

"Good job," he said, but I couldn't stop frowning. I felt horrible knowing that I had disappointed one of our fans, and wished we could have finished out our set like we planned.

When Portia arrived backstage a few minutes later, she could read the frustration on my face as I packed away my guitar. "Tenney, you look mopier than a hound dog when it rains," she said.

"I can't help it," I grumbled. "It was barely a show."

"At least we played pretty well," Logan pointed out.

"That really doesn't make me feel better," I shot back.

A flash of tension bristled between us.

Portia turned to Zane and Dad. "Gentlemen, can y'all grant me a little time with my favorite duo?"

"Sure," Zane said.

"We'll take the guitars back to the van," Dad told me. "How about y'all come meet us there in twenty minutes?"

"Okay," I said.

As Dad and Zane disappeared into the crowd, Portia put a hand on her hip and looked us over. "I know just what you two need," she said. "Follow me."

It turned out what we needed was hot chocolate, velvety and sweet and topped with whipped cream in tall, striped cups. Portia got them for us at a coffee shop

THE SOUND OF SILENCE

a few blocks up Main Street, and sat down with us at a rickety table in the corner to talk about our show.

"You two did remarkably well, given the sound catastrophe," Portia said.

"Exactly," Logan agreed, but I shook my head.

"But we were only just getting into our groove when we had to stop," I insisted gloomily.

"You played the show, Tenney," Portia cut in. "That's all that counts when you're on tour. You can't worry about too much else."

She set down her hot chocolate and looked from me to Logan and back with a laser-sharp stare.

"Being on tour is tough," she continued. "Sometimes your sets will be great. Other times, not so much. You can't worry about any of that. You just have to keep going. Don't get rattled, don't worry about what you can't change. Just try your hardest and think on your feet. Think of it this way: Now you can go to your next show knowing that you already got your rough patch out of the way."

I looked up at her. "But Belle Starr told me that the first show sets the tone for the rest of the tour. What if—"

Portia waved her hand as if she was sweeping away my worry. "No matter how badly a performance goes, always remember that your next show could be your best show. You just need to keep your head in the game and be there for each other. Okay?"

Logan and I nodded.

I'm not sure if it was Portia's pep talk or the sugar rush from the hot chocolate, but by the time we walked out of the coffee shop into the crisp December air, I felt a whole lot better.

"Well, this is where we say our farewells," Portia said, giving us both hugs. "You know where to find Zane's van?"

"The van's just up there," Logan said, pointing to the side street ahead.

"All right then. I won't wish you luck, 'cause you don't need it," Portia declared. "You've got talent, grit, and determination. And *that* is enough to make any tour a success. Take it from someone who knows."

We grinned and said our good-byes.

"Send me some photos from the road—and remember what I said!" Portia called as she walked off. And with a wave back at us, she melted into the crowd.

As Logan and I started walking back to the van, I repeated Portia's words in my head like a mantra: *Keep your head in the game, Tenney. Our next show could be our best show.* I sure hoped she was right.

ON THE ROAD

Chapter 8

Once we got on the highway, Zane put on a CD. By the time the zesty twang of bluegrass music filled the van, Franklin was fading into the distance.

Outside, patches of half-melted snow and skeletal trees dotted the landscape. I pressed my nose to the window's cold glass, my breath fogging up the view. We were headed to Knoxville, a medium-sized city on the eastern side of the state. It was nearly two hundred miles away, so the drive was going to take a while. I'd never been to Knoxville, so I was really excited to visit. Still, after a few minutes of passing billboards, barns, and cold-looking cows, I started to get bored.

I opened my backpack, looking for something to do. *I could write a new holiday song!* I realized with a

zip of enthusiasm. *Yes! I'll write something fun that I can sing at the holiday jam.*

I pulled out my songwriting journal, where I keep all my notes and ideas for songs. I turned to a new page and stared at it, resting my head against the window. I had no room to get out my guitar to tinker around with melodies. So I tried to come up with lyrics instead. I wrote down a few holiday words, trying to spark inspiration: *holly, Santa Claus, mistletoe, sleigh bells* . . . But with Dad and Zane chatting in front, and Logan's knee bouncing as he sat beside me, it was hard to concentrate.

I glanced at Logan. He was hunched over his phone, typing.

"What are you doing?" I asked.

"Texting," he said impatiently, as if I should have known better than to ask.

I jiggled the sleep out of my foot and looked around. "Want to play a game?" I asked, trying to get him to lighten up. "My family always plays I spy when we go on road trips. It'll be fun!"

Logan grunted. I took that as a yes.

"Okay, I'll go first," I said, spotting a highway sign advertising AUNTIE EM'S PIES! 2 MILES! "I spy with my little eye something delicious!"

"I'm busy," Logan said, without looking up from his phone.

"Are you sure?" I said, giving him a friendly nudge.

He looked up, startled. "What? Yes," he said tersely, then refocused on his phone.

Annoyance prickled through me, but I shook it off. Whatever. Logan wasn't in the mood to play games, apparently.

"How much longer till we get there?" I asked.

Dad glanced over his shoulder. "Long enough that you should probably stop asking," he said with a wink.

I sighed again, huddling deeper in my coat for warmth. My eyelids felt heavy. *I'll just close them for a minute*, I thought. *Then I'll keep working on the holiday song.*

The next thing I knew, Dad was shaking me awake.

"Wake up, sleepy," he said. "We're here."

ON THE ROAD

Our hotel was on the outskirts of Knoxville, on a big landscaped hill overlooking the highway. As we pulled up the circular driveway to the front entrance, a wave of excitement hit me. The last time I'd stayed in a hotel was when I was ten and we went on a family vacation to Florida. Seeing the hotel really brought it home to me that we were on tour. I think Logan felt the same way, because when we got out of the van he kept looking around like he was afraid he was going to miss something.

"They have vending machines and a snack bar," he pointed out as we wheeled our suitcases into the lobby. "Do you think they have a pool?"

For the first time since we left Franklin, Logan cracked a hopeful smile.

"They don't, unfortunately," Zane chimed in. "But they do have a business center."

I squinted at him, confused. "That's no fun!"

"It is for *me*!" Zane cracked with a loopy grin, which made us laugh.

After check-in, we took the elevator to the third floor, where our rooms were. Dad and I were sharing one room while Zane and Logan had another a few doors down. As we walked down the hall, my whole body buzzed with excitement. In Florida, I remembered, there had been complimentary chocolate chip cookies waiting for us in our room, and big fluffy pillows that Aubrey and I had used in a pillow fight.

Dad slipped the key card into the lock and the door clicked open. Inside, the room was large and neat, with two beds with purple-and-gold bedspreads and matching carpet. It was nice, but in a business-like way. There definitely weren't any chocolate chip cookies. I set my bags down and poked at one of the flat pillows.

"Want to call home?" Dad asked.

I perked up. That was exactly what I needed right now.

Dad laughed, handing me the phone. After a few rings, Mom picked up the video call. "Tenney!"

"Hi, Mom!" I said. I had only been away from home for half a day and I already missed her.

I had to smile when Aubrey and Mason crowded into the frame with Mom on-screen.

ON THE ROAD

"How's it going?" Mason asked, but Aubrey interrupted before I could reply.

"It's amazing, right?! I bet it's incredible," she declared, breathless. "You're on tour!"

"Y-yeah," I fumbled, trying to match my sister's enthusiasm. "It's really great." I told them about our audio snags at the Franklin show, doing my best to downplay the disaster and sound as optimistic as possible. But I didn't want to sound like I was complaining, so I changed the subject. "What did you guys do today?" I asked.

"I made Waylon a reindeer antler headband for the Howl-iday Ramble," Aubrey told me. "And Mom and I practiced 'The Holly and the Ivy' for the jam. We decided Mom should play Autoharp and not mandolin."

Aubrey continued chattering a mile a minute, telling me all about their first "rehearsal." As she and Mom teased each other about missed cues and shaky harmonies, I felt a twinge of regret that I wasn't home with them. But I shrugged it off.

You're on tour! I reminded myself. *That's a*

thousand times more exciting than rehearsing for the family holiday jam.

Aubrey was still talking when someone knocked on the door. Dad hopped off the bed, glanced through the peephole, and opened the door.

"Hey," Logan said, waving at me from the doorway.

"Wait, who's that? Who's there?" Aubrey bleated on the other end as Mason and Mom laughed.

"It's Logan, hold on," I told her.

"This is a bad time," Logan said, looking self-conscious.

"No, it's okay," Dad said, coming over to the doorway, but Logan was already shaking his head.

"It's fine, never mind," he said, taking a step back. "I'll just see you guys tomorrow." Before I could reply, Logan walked off.

Dad looked at me and shrugged.

After a few more minutes on the phone, Dad and I said our good-byes and I love yous to Mom, Mason, and Aubrey and hung up.

Dad stood up, bouncing on his heels.

ON THE ROAD

"Boy, I am wired from sitting in the van so long," he said. "I'm gonna go stretch my legs before dinner. Want to come?"

I shook my head. Talking to my family on the phone had energized me, and suddenly, a song lyric popped into my head.

"You go ahead," I said, pulling out my songwriting notebook. "I'm feeling inspired."

"Okay, then," Dad said with a wink. "I'll be back. Call or text if you need me."

I nodded and scribbled down the lyric before I could forget it. As soon as he left, I crossed the room and snapped open my guitar case. Slipping the strap overhead and across my shoulders, I moved to an armchair and settled in.

I sang the lyric first, the tune coming naturally as if I had known the song for years. Then I strummed out a few chords that complemented the melody, and from there I figured out the chord progression to form the first verse. It was pretty and yearning, like a ballad. I liked it, but it wasn't exactly overflowing with Christmas cheer.

TENNEY

By the time I found a basic structure for the song that I really liked, the door opened and Dad popped his head in.

"Ready to eat?" he said. "I thought we could order room service."

Was it time for dinner already? I often lose sense of time when my songwriting is going well. I peered out the window, and sure enough, a cheery coral-and-pumpkin sunset filled the sky.

"Yes!" I said, suddenly realizing I was starving.

As I set down my guitar, a calm pride surged through me, the way it always does after I've cracked a song's structure. It wasn't done yet, but it was a solid start. Most importantly, working on it had lifted my spirits, making me feel like everything that lay ahead was bright with promise.

BREAKING
THE ICE

Chapter 9

*T*he next morning, Dad and I met Logan and
Zane in the diner downstairs and ordered
breakfast. By the time my waffles and bacon arrived,
my stomach was growling like a stray cat. I poured
syrup over my plate and dug in.

As we ate, Zane went over the plan for the concert, which was scheduled for later that morning at
Knoxville's main library. "Our show's part of their
annual holiday music series," Zane told us. "They've
been doing it for a few years now to promote the
library and help bring the community together."

"We're playing at a *library*?" Logan said uncer-
tainly. "I hope they don't expect us to play quietly."

"Not at all," Zane said with a chuckle. "We'll be
performing in the front lobby, actually. They set up a
stage and speakers there, and seating, and they

handle all the audio. All we need to do is show up with our instruments."

"Great," Dad said, but remembering the audio disaster during our Franklin show, worry tied a knot in my stomach.

"I think we should go through our set list again, and talk about what songs we'd cut if we run out of time again," I told Logan. "Just so we can be prepared if something goes wrong."

I expected Logan to agree with me, but instead he wrinkled his nose.

"I doubt we're going to have any more problems," he said, taking a bite of his breakfast burrito.

Irritation flickered inside me, but I squelched it. "We can't know that for sure," I pointed out, then turned to Zane and Dad. "Don't you think we need to have a plan for what to do if we need to make changes mid-show?"

Logan bristled, but Zane jumped in before he could reply. "Tenney's got a good point," he said. "We've got some time before we need to leave for the show. I need to go make some calls about our upcoming gigs after this. While I do that, y'all can figure out a shorter set list as a backup."

"We can do that," I replied, relieved that Zane agreed with me.

Logan stayed silent and stabbed a sausage patty with his fork. I eyed him, confused. He was acting as if I had just suggested that we totally overhaul our set list. *Maybe he's just not a morning person*, I decided.

After breakfast, Dad and Zane went back to our rooms as Logan and I sat on couches in the lobby to work on a shortened set list.

I pulled out my songwriting notebook and a pen and glanced at Logan. He didn't look like he was in the mood to work on anything. He had his headphones on and his hoodie pulled down over his head as he stared at his phone.

"So what songs do you think we would skip if we had to?" I asked.

"Whatever ones you want," Logan said with a shrug, still looking at his phone. He started typing a text and sent it off with a *whoosh*.

"Really?" I asked.

Logan nodded. "I trust you," he said quietly, but he still didn't make eye contact.

"Um, okay," I said. It felt strange to revise the set list without talking it out, so I ran through each song, telling Logan which ones I thought we could leave out.

I expected that he would object to skipping one song or another, but he didn't. He just nodded like he was barely listening to me. I squinted at him. The Logan I knew always had an opinion about everything, especially when it came to our music.

"Are you even listening to me?" I asked finally.

"Yes," he said sharply.

I frowned. Logan's gaze flickered up at me for a brief moment before returning to his phone.

"You want to skip a few holiday songs and make sure we always keep 'Reach the Sky' as our last song," he said, softening his voice. "That's fine. Whatever."

"Okay," I said. I waited for Logan to say

something more, but it was clear that we were done. I shrank into the corner of the couch, annoyed.

I remembered feeling this way before, when Logan and I first started working together earlier this year. Logan had been stressed out trying to balance band rehearsals and songwriting sessions with his responsibilities at home, and he was in a bad mood *all* the time. It made collaborating on our music almost impossible. Logan even quit the band for a little while! But since then, we had become a team.

So why was he shutting me out now?

I looked around. It was almost noon, and the lobby was nearly empty. Besides Logan and me, there were a few travelers looking at their phones, but that was it. Despite the cheery holiday decorations, the place felt lonely.

We had been gone for only a day, but all of a sudden, I really missed my friends. *I wonder what Jaya and Holliday are doing right now,* I thought. *Probably something fun.* My heart sank a little.

I sat up, trying to shake off my melancholy.

TENNEY

Pulling out my phone, I took a photo of the lobby and sent it to my friends.

Guys! This is our hotel in Knoxville!

I waited for an excited response, but no one answered, so I typed another text.

More pix to come! How are you doing?

I stared at my phone. I thought for sure that someone would text back immediately, but my phone stayed silent.

When nobody had texted back a few minutes later, I was officially antsy. I wished it was time to head to the Knoxville library now, but we didn't have to leave for another half hour. I glanced at Logan again, who was *still* staring at his phone. I only lasted about thirty seconds until I jumped to my feet.

"Let's do something fun," I said decisively to Logan.

He squinted at me, pulling off his headphones. "Like what?"

"I have no idea," I replied. "But I bet we can figure something out."

I made a face and Logan laughed despite himself. Then I gave him my biggest, brightest smile. I wasn't sure why Logan was in such a funk, but I was determined to pull him out of it. I yanked him to his feet before he could protest.

"Okay, fine," Logan relented. "Let's go have fun."

As we circled the large lobby looking for something to do, I texted my dad to let him know that we were going to explore the hotel. We found a pair of automatic massage chairs and tried sitting in them, but it wasn't relaxing at all. Instead, it felt like someone was dragging bumpy carrots up and down my back. I pressed a different button and my chair started vibrating so strongly I thought I would be shaken out of my seat.

"*Gonna be mys-e-e-e-elf, nobody e-e-e-else!*" I sang, my voice quivering. "*Gonna reach the sky-y-y-y if I only try-y-y-y!*"

Logan laughed so hard his face turned red. "You sound like a robot!"

I pressed the OFF button and giggled. "Maybe we should bring these chairs to our show at the library!" I joked.

He scrunched his nose, and then smiled earnestly. "This was fun," he said. "Thanks for getting me off the couch."

"You're welcome," I said.

Logan started to say something, then hesitated. His face looked just like it had when he showed up at our hotel room door last night. I waited for him to try again, but he just stared at his shoes.

"I'm sorry I couldn't talk when you came by yesterday," I offered, trying to coax him to open up.

Logan's cheeks turned beet red, like I'd caught him making a mistake.

"What? Oh, that's fine," he said uneasily.

"Logan, is everything okay?" I asked, taking a more direct approach.

He looked up at me, but before he could say anything we heard Dad calling our names. A second later, Dad rounded the corner, out of breath.

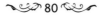

BREAKING THE ICE

"There you are!" he said. He checked his watch. "The van's all packed up. We need to get going or you'll be late for your show!"

Logan hopped up eagerly. "Yeah, let's go!" he said.

I stood up, disappointed that Logan and I hadn't been able to finish our conversation. But I shook it off as we hustled to the van—we had a show to play!

CHANGE OF PLANS

Chapter 10

*J*t took only a few minutes to drive to downtown Knoxville, but my heart was already jitterbugging with anticipation when we pulled up to the main library.

"Let's check out the space and then get set up," Zane said, looking at his watch.

As I unbuckled my seat belt and looked up at the blocky cement building, I suddenly felt a little nervous. *Keep your head in the game*, I reminded myself. *Your next show could be your best show!* Chilly air hit my face as I stepped out of the van, excitement tingling through me. I couldn't wait to get inside the library and start warming up. I grabbed my guitar, hurried up the front steps, went through the glass doors . . . and stopped cold.

The lobby was full of people. Not just people,

children. An entire busload of eight-year-olds—dressed identically in red-and-green uniforms—talking and fidgeting and looking overwhelmed as they struggled onto a wide set of risers under a banner reading WELCOME EASTERN TENNESSEE CHILDREN'S CHOIR!

Logan and I glanced at each other, then at Dad and Zane. They looked as confused as I felt.

"What's going on?" I asked.

"Let me go find out," Zane said, and went to the front desk. Dad squeezed my shoulder reassuringly and followed behind him.

I felt a gentle tap on my shoulder, and turned around.

A trio of girls stood in front of me. They all had the same sandy-colored hair and wide, awed expressions, and so I figured they must be sisters.

"You're Tenney Grant!" the youngest sister said breathlessly. She looked like she was around Aubrey's age.

"Um . . . yes?" I said, so surprised that my answer came out sounding like a question.

"And you're Logan?!" the middle girl said without missing a beat.

"Yeah," Logan said warily.

"Wow!" the middle girl said triumphantly, with an excited little hop.

"I'm Emily Hayden, and these are my sisters, Sophie and Corinne," the oldest girl said. "We watched the video of y'all performing 'Reach the Sky' with Belle Starr about a thousand times, so when we heard you were playing in Knoxville, we just got so excited—"

"Our mom drove us all the way from Russellville to see you!" the littlest one, Corinne, blurted.

"We're just so excited to see y'all," Emily said over her.

"And to hear you perform in person," finished Sophie.

They bobbed their heads at us, beaming, and I smiled back. Knowing they'd taken a special trip to see us made me want to play the best show ever for them.

"Wow! Nice to meet you!" I said. At least, I *tried* to say that, but the children's choir had started vocal-izing, drowning me out.

"Are you playing with the choir?" Emily asked.

CHANGE OF PLANS

Logan and I exchanged an uncertain look.

"We don't really know!" I admitted.

Dad and Zane appeared on the far side of the lobby, talking to a tiny woman with a big clipboard. The moment I saw Zane's face, I could tell something was wrong. I'd never seen him so serious before. We told the Hayden sisters we'd be right back.

"What's wrong?" I asked, worried. Zane looked from Logan to me and back, like he was trying to pick his words carefully.

"Apparently," he said at last, "you're not scheduled to play today."

"What?" Logan and I said at the same time, loud enough to make the Hayden sisters look over at us.

"I'll let Mrs. Colvin explain," Zane said, gesturing to the woman beside him, who wore big glasses and a mortified expression. "She's the managing librarian."

"Y-yes, well, we are just so sorry about this," stammered Mrs. Colvin. "The director of our music series had to leave town due to a family emergency a while ago, and we've been trying to pick up the pieces, but everyone's been so busy with the holidays . . ." She trailed off, her face darkening into the color of a ripe beet. "When we rearranged the concert schedule a few weeks ago, it appears that we accidentally double-booked."

"That is how it appears," Dad said coolly.

I twisted my hair nervously. The director of the children's choir came over to us. As all the adults started discussing what to do about the situation, my gaze drifted over to the sisters. They were talking to other people, but kept looking in our direction excitedly.

Finally, I found my voice. "People came to see us," I said. "They expect us to play. I don't want to let them down."

"Neither do I," Logan agreed.

The children's choir director, a Latino man in a candy-cane-striped bow tie, gave us a sympathetic smile. "How about this?" he suggested. "Our kids have been rehearsing for six weeks, so we can't give you our whole show slot. But you could play a few songs with us at the end."

"Really?" Zane said.

CHANGE OF PLANS

"Absolutely," the choir director said with a firm nod.

I managed a smile back, but inside I was still struggling. Judging from Logan's expression, I could tell he was, too. This was supposed to be the second show of our tour, and once again, we weren't going to be able to play a whole set.

"I know this isn't what we expected, guys, but the alternative is no concert at all," Zane told us quietly, like he could read our minds.

"I know," I said. I turned to the choir director. "Thank you for being so generous," I told him.

"Of course," he said simply. "That's the spirit of the season, after all."

For the next ten minutes, we all worked together to figure out which songs Logan and I could perform with the choir. There wasn't any room for Logan's drum set in the space, but he could play his guitar.

When it was time for the show to begin almost all the chairs set up for the audience were taken. Mrs. Colvin added four extra chairs to the front row for Logan, Zane, Dad, and me. We sat down just as the choir director stepped up in front of the risers and raised his hands to quiet the squealing children. They responded quickly, looking forward and hushing anyone who was still chattering. A pianist played a short intro and the children began to sing "Rockin' Around the Christmas Tree."

They were overflowing with enthusiasm and holiday cheer, and my spirits couldn't help but lift as I watched them perform song after song. By the time we were supposed to join them onstage, my hands hurt from clapping so hard.

"Now we'd like to welcome up some special guests," said the choir director. "Tenney Grant and Logan Everett!"

Logan and I brought up our guitars in front of the choir as the children squealed with surprise.

"Cool!" said a little boy in the choir, his eyes sparkling as he looked at Logan's guitar.

First, we sang "Winter Wonderland" with the choir. Then Logan and I played "Jingle Bells" and the kids sang along at the chorus. Since we hadn't had time to rehearse with them, it wasn't perfect, but we sounded pretty good, and I was glad that the

CHANGE OF PLANS

Tenney & Logan fans who'd shown up got to hear us play.

When we finished, we got a round of applause and a bunch of hugs from some of the choir kids and our fans. But no one was more excited than the Hayden sisters. They bought an EP and got Zane to take a bunch of photos of all of us together.

"Thank you so much for coming," I said gratefully, between snaps. I felt bad that they'd made a special trip just to hear us play two songs.

"We loved it! You guys were so good!" Emily said, beaming. "I just wish you could have played more."

"If you guys aren't busy tomorrow, they're playing a whole set at the civic auditorium in Kingsport," Zane chimed in.

Sophie's face lit up. "Really?! That's pretty close to us!" she said, yanking Emily's arm. "We should ask Mom if we can go!"

"Maybe," Emily said, but she looked uncertain.

"How about I give y'all some free tickets?" Zane suggested. "For you three and your mom, as our way of thanking you for coming out today."

Emily and Sophie looked surprised and happy, and Corinne whooped in excitement.

"NO WAY!" she yelled, hopping up and down, and threw herself around Zane's legs.

"I'll take that to mean you're interested in the tickets," he said, laughing.

Corinne squealed, and we all laughed.

"Please come," I said. I wanted the Haydens to get to see a *real* Tenney & Logan concert.

"We'll definitely try to make it," Emily replied, beaming.

"Well, I'd say that ended up being a lot of fun, against all odds," Dad said as Zane started the engine.

"That's life on tour," Zane offered. "Nothing ever happens the way you expect."

"It would be so great if the Haydens came to the show tomorrow, right?" I said to Logan, who was looking out the window.

"Sure," Logan said flatly.

CHANGE OF PLANS

"Logan, they're our fans!" I chided. "Can you at least pretend you're excited?"

He threw me a sharp look.

Annoyance stung me, but I stifled it. I had no idea why Logan was suddenly in such a grumpy mood, but I wasn't going to let it ruin my excitement. I turned my thoughts to tomorrow's show in Kingsport.

"The auditorium in Kingsport's pretty big, right?" I asked.

"Yep," Dad said.

"They can fit up to eight hundred people inside," Zane added.

"Wow," I said. Logan and I had played for a bigger crowd at Belle's concert . . . but imagine if that many people showed up to *our* show! I turned to Logan. "We need to be really on point tomorrow. Every song needs to *rock*."

Logan didn't say anything. He was staring at his phone like I wasn't even in the van. My annoyance ignited into full-on irritation.

"Did you hear what I said?" I asked, an edge creeping into my voice.

"Of course I did," Logan snapped. "You don't need to talk about how good the shows need to be, Tenney. I get it. I just want to get on with the tour."

I blinked hard. I felt like Logan had just told me to shut up. My feelings were hurt, but I just rolled my eyes and turned my back on him.

Dad and Zane exchanged a concerned look.

"Take it down a notch, y'all," Dad told us gently.

"Right," Zane said in his laid-back way. "No need to fuss about something until there's something to fuss about."

I shrugged, making sure to ignore Logan. I got out my headphones and found some music on my phone, then put on a song loud enough to drown out the angry hurt I was feeling.

I don't know what Logan's problem is, I thought. *But from now on, I'm just going to focus on playing the best music I can . . . with or without him.*

UNDER PRESSURE

Chapter 11

*J*ust outside Kingsport, we stopped for dinner at a barbecue restaurant, a squat brick building with a live honky-tonk band and air that smelled of hickory smoke. The food and the music were both great, but it was hard to enjoy them because I was still so annoyed with Logan. He didn't say much during the meal beyond asking our server for the Wi-Fi password. Mostly, he checked his phone and stuffed his face as if he was in an eating contest.

It was dusk when we reached our hotel. When I opened up the van door, I gasped. The chilly evening breeze had morphed into an ugly, freezing wind. It blew into the van so fiercely that I worried we might blow away like leaves, even though I knew better. By the time I stepped into the revolving door, I felt like I was made of ice.

TENNEY

A festive Christmas tree glittered in the lobby, alongside a table stocked with hot cider and cookies. It was toasty and cozy, and I was glad to be there and not in the van with grumpy Logan, who was now huddled on the lobby couch with his eyes glued to his cell phone.

I checked my own phone and noticed that I'd received a few texts from Jaya.

We miss you!! read the first one. She'd attached a selfie of her and Holliday making pouty "sad" faces to the camera.

But we are trying to survive, read the next text. This time, the photo was of Jaya and Holliday drinking hot chocolates and grinning with whipped cream mustaches. I had to laugh.

There were more photos. Jaya and Holliday at the mall. Jaya and Holliday posing in front of the gigantic Christmas tree at Centennial Park. Jaya and Holliday wearing matching elf hats, laughing. Each picture made me smile, but it also made me wish I was home.

Looks super fun! I wrote back, but my heart felt heavy. *I miss you guys, too.*

UNDER PRESSURE

I sent the text and waited for Jaya to write back, but my phone stayed quiet. Sitting there, with my guitar case at my feet, I felt a long pang of homesickness.

I squinted at my guitar case, trying to think of what I could do to take my mind off missing home. *Maybe we could go bowling!* I thought. I loved bowling with Dad. Grabbing my guitar, I stood up and headed over to where Dad and Zane were waiting to check in. As I reached them, I caught a snippet of their conversation.

". . . and I don't think they're handling the road too well," Zane was saying.

Dad nodded. "They get under each other's skin. And being on tour seems to be making things worse."

I froze, realizing they were talking about me and Logan.

Zane shook his head. "I'm worried that whatever's going on between the two of them offstage will follow them onstage. If that happens, I've gotta wonder if they're really ready to make an album together," Zane said, handing Dad a room key. "They could implode before we even start recording."

"I hear you," Dad said, letting out a sigh.

I hadn't realized that the tension between me and Logan was worrying Zane so much. Had we already blown our chance to make a record without realizing it? Or was there still hope that Zane could change his mind? I wasn't sure, but I knew I needed to talk to Logan about it *now*.

I made a beeline for the couch, but Logan was gone. I spotted him clicking around on his phone by the elevators, the hood up on his winter coat. I walked up to him and tapped him on the shoulder. He spun around, startled. I saw a flash of his little brother's face on his phone's screen, and realized he was on a video call.

Logan retreated, holding up his finger to show me he needed a minute. He turned away, lowered his voice, and kept talking. After a minute, I heard him say, "I'll see you in a couple of days, I promise."

He hung up and turned back to me, his mouth clamped into a worried line.

UNDER PRESSURE

"Are you okay?" I asked.

"I'm fine," he said abruptly, pushing his hood off his head. "Jude keeps saying he wants me to come home."

I couldn't really tell if Logan was sad or angry. It seemed like he was both, which made it tough to figure out what to say. I started to speak, but Logan pocketed his phone and pushed past me.

Irritation jolted through me, and I struggled to keep my temper in check. Logan was clearly stressed out about something, I thought, but telling him that we might have blown our chance to record an album wasn't going to make him feel any better. I decided not to tell Logan what I'd overheard . . . at least not right now.

I followed Logan back to the lobby. As we all rolled our suitcases to the elevators together, Dad and Zane studied our faces. I looked over at Logan, who just looked bored. I gave them my biggest smile, hoping to convince them that everything was fine—even though everything was definitely *not* fine.

TENNEY

Once we were in the room, I put on my pajamas while Dad found a movie on TV. As we watched, I had to stop myself from turning to him to talk about what I'd heard. But I didn't want him to think I'd been eavesdropping on him and Zane on purpose. When the credits finally started rolling, I turned off the light by my bed and tried to fall asleep.

It didn't work. I couldn't stop mulling over what Zane had said. The thought that Logan and I might never get to record the songs we'd worked so hard to create really upset me. I exhaled, turning over for the millionth time.

"Everything okay, sweetheart?" Dad said from his bed.

I hesitated. I wanted to talk to Dad, but I knew that it wouldn't do any good. After all, *Zane* was the one I needed to convince that Logan and I were ready to make a record. So I just said, "I'm having trouble winding down."

"Well, tomorrow's a big show," Dad said. "Just try and clear your mind."

He switched off his light, and I nestled into my

pillow, turning over. But as I stared into the blackness, my mind was far from clear.

We have three shows left, I reasoned to myself. *Logan and I need to be great at all of them. Starting tomorrow, we need to prove ourselves to Zane all over again.*

GET IT TOGETHER

Chapter 12

*M*y head ached when I woke up the next morning, as if worrying had kept my forehead scrunched up all night. I slung my legs off the bed and sat up. The room was chilly. I moved to a window covered in thick patches of starry frost, and pressed my nose against a clear spot. In the parking lot outside, people fought the wind as they tramped to their cars, their breath hanging in frozen clouds around them.

Once I'd showered and dressed, Dad and I met Logan and Zane at the hotel restaurant downstairs for breakfast.

"Today should be a nice break for you two. You don't play until one o'clock this afternoon, which leaves some time for you to relax," Zane said as we finished up our pancakes and bacon.

GET IT TOGETHER

I glanced at the clock on my phone. It wasn't even ten o'clock.

"What should we do until the show?" I asked.

Zane handed the server his credit card and checked his phone. "Up to you," he said. "I need to work for a little bit after this. I'm still double-checking details for tomorrow."

"Maybe we can walk around and go check out Kingsport," I suggested to Dad and Logan.

Logan looked at me in disbelief. "Are you kidding? It's T-minus freezing out there."

"So?" I said, a little defiantly. "It could still be fun."

After breakfast, Dad and I headed for the hotel's sliding front entrance. The moment we stepped outside, however, bitter, thrashing wind beat us back into the lobby, teeth chattering. *So much for exploring Kingsport*, I thought in frustration.

Dad shrugged. "Why don't you and Logan work on a new song?" he asked.

"Good idea," I said. *Or maybe this would be a good time to talk to Logan about what Zane told Dad*, I thought.

I found Logan settled in a lobby chair, head-phones on. I sat down in the chair next to his.

"Hey," I said.

He didn't respond so I poked him in the arm. He looked up and pulled out an earbud.

"I have to tell you something," I whispered.

"What?" he said, his voice sharp. "I'm busy."

I felt like steam was about to shoot out my ears. But then I spotted Dad rifling through a stack of magazines across the lobby, and took a deep, calm-ing breath. The last thing Logan and I needed was for Dad to witness another argument before our next show.

Logan waved his hand in front of me. "Earth to Tenney," he said impatiently. "Were you going to tell me something or not?"

"Never mind," I said. I stood up and left him alone.

For the next hour, I tried to entertain myself. I wandered around the hotel taking a video, and sent it to Jaya, Holliday, and my family so they could see what I was up to. I played games on my phone and listened to music, but even after listening to a whole album of Patsy Cline B-sides, I still had time to kill. *I never realized going on tour involved so much waiting,* I thought. In my imagination, I'd pictured myself exploring cool places, taking photos, eating new foods. But so far, I hadn't had a chance to do too much of that.

Bored out of my mind, I finally went back to our hotel room.

"Hey there," Dad said, looking up from his laptop as I came in. "Did you and Logan manage to write your next big hit?"

I smiled, but changed the subject.

"What are you doing?" I asked, walking over.

"I was just checking out how many views your 'Reach the Sky' videos have gotten," he said, standing up to stretch. "This one's gotten nearly forty thousand now."

"Really?" I said, peering over his shoulder at the computer screen.

"Zane put a link underneath it to your tour website," Dad said, pointing it out. "And the views have actually picked up since the tour started, which is good. I bet we're going to see quite a crowd at today's show. It was definitely the right call to do a tour now."

Except now you and Zane aren't sure that we're ready to cut an album, I thought silently. A big crowd at today's show would be great, but it also meant more pressure on me and Logan. We *had* to be incredible. I stood up, feeling my stomach tighten in a nervous knot.

"You okay?" Dad asked, cocking a curious eyebrow at me.

"Yes, I'm fine," I said, as confidently as I could. The last thing I needed was Dad telling Zane that I was anxious. That could be just another mark against me. "I should get ready."

I changed into my show outfit, put on simple stage makeup and pulled my hair into a thick French side braid. By the time I put on the guitar-pick necklace that Aubrey had made for me, it was time to get going.

"How long do we have for sound check?" I asked as Zane turned onto the highway.

"Ten or fifteen minutes," Zane replied.

GET IT TOGETHER

"Any way we can get longer?" I asked.

"Why would we need any longer?" Logan asked me, frowning. "We've been rehearsing for weeks—our set is tight."

"I just feel like we could use a little extra time to warm up today," I said, as evenly as I could. "It couldn't hurt."

Logan shook his head. "Don't overthink it," he said. "We just need to get through the set."

I stared at him in disbelief. *Ugh!* Every ounce of me wanted to shake Logan and lecture him about how crucial this show was, but I couldn't do that in front of Dad and Zane.

We turned onto a wide, tree-lined street. As the van slowed down, I looked out my window. The view made me gasp in surprise. A crowd of preteens bundled in hats and coats against the cold waited to get inside. There must have been around fifty of them trailing from the auditorium's front doors down the steps to the white marquee sign out front. A cluster of girls took a photo of themselves next to the sign that announced TODAY @ 1:00 P.M.: TENNEY & LOGAN HOLIDAY CONCERT!

"Whoa," Logan said, leaning over my shoulder to see through the window. "Are they waiting for *us*?"

"Yes, sir," Zane said with a lopsided grin. "You see? Word's getting out about you two."

Zane pulled around to the rear of the building, so that we could enter out of sight from the audience. We'd barely parked when a pair of auditorium technicians swarmed us and started unloading gear from the back of the van. I caught a glimpse of satisfaction on Logan's face. Finally, he was getting the crew he had been hoping for.

Maybe that will cheer him up, I thought.

Inside, the auditorium stage manager showed us to the dressing rooms, where we left our guitars. As soon as we got settled, we tuned our instruments and hit the stage for sound check. The stage was huge, nearly as wide as the Ryman Auditorium's. Zane was already onstage when we arrived, setting up Logan's drum kit.

Sound check felt like it passed in a heartbeat. Logan and I didn't talk much to each other; we were both focused on our instruments. Finally, Dad and Zane went offstage, leaving us alone.

GET IT TOGETHER

I stepped over to my double microphone. Although I couldn't see the audience because the curtain was closed, I could hear a hubbub of voices on the other side. My stomach clenched with a sudden burst of nerves.

"How many people are out there?" I asked the stage manager.

"Last time I checked, they'd sold nearly three hundred tickets," he replied.

An icy, electric thrill charged through me. It was the biggest audience we had played for yet—by a long shot. *This could be our first great concert on tour!* I realized.

I glanced at Logan. He was sitting motionless behind his kit, sticks in hand, but his expression looked like he was a million miles away. It made me nervous.

"Hey," I said softly. His eyes met mine.

In that moment, I had another urge to tell him what I had overheard, that Zane was losing faith in us, that this show, more than any other one we'd ever played together, had to be *amazing* if we wanted to ensure that we still had a shot at making a record. But I was too scared to say all that so close to going on.

Instead I just blurted, "This show's really important."

Logan gave me a squinty, confused look. "*Every* show is important," he told me.

"Yeah, but this show—" I started. But just then, the audience grew quiet as a voice boomed over the intercom.

"Ladies and gentlemen, please welcome, all the way from Music City, USA, Tenney and Logan!"

The audience cheered, and my heart started beating double time.

The stage manager signaled that the curtain was going up and the work lights above us turned off. In the dark, my whole body felt electrified. Then the stage lights came up, fast and bright. I wobbled and caught my microphone stand with one hand, steadying myself, as Logan launched into our first song, an energetic rock version of "Deck the Halls."

We were strong and quick for the first four measures. Then Logan's drumming got messy. His tempo kept shifting. At first he was too fast, but when I shot him a look he overcorrected and got too slow before we finally fell back in sync. We finished the song okay and the audience clapped enthusiastically, but the smile on my face felt glued on. Underneath, I was anxious.

By now my eyes had adjusted, and I could see there was a good-sized audience in the cavernous room. Along with a few adults, most of the crowd were kids roughly the same age as me and Logan.

"Thank you so much," I told them. "We're thrilled to be here."

I paused, waiting for Logan to kick into our next song, but he didn't.

I glanced over. Behind his drums, Logan was looking at me expectantly, as if I was supposed to do something. I raised my eyebrows and he snapped to it, starting in on the rhythmic intro to "Carolina Highway."

A few measures in, Logan fell off-tempo again. He missed a cue on his verse solo, came in late, and messed up the lyrics.

When the song was over, I turned to Logan.

"What is going on?" I hissed at him under my breath as the crowd cheered. "You're falling apart!"

Logan sneered. "I made one mistake," he said, bristling. "You're overreacting."

"You made *three* mistakes, and I'm *not* overreacting!" I snapped.

Logan rolled his eyes, and peppery anger flared in my chest. I took a deep breath and resisted the urge to yell at Logan in front of the entire audience.

"Just . . . get it together," I told him as politely as I could. The applause died down, and I turned back to the audience with a smile. I realized I was clenching my guitar in an iron grip. I forced open my fingers and stretched them, trying to breathe calmly.

The rest of the show went by in a blur. Logan stopped having tempo problems, so we sounded better. Still, after our argument it was hard for me to enjoy playing. Even though we sounded great, we could hardly look each other in the eye. Much to my relief, the audience seemed to be enjoying the music. Their applause grew louder after each song.

When it was time to perform "Cold Creek Christmas," Logan grabbed his guitar off its stand by

GET IT TOGETHER

the drum kit and moved to a microphone beside me. We stood side by side and played the song from start to finish perfectly, our guitars and voices blending into one shimmering sound. We sounded beautiful, but all I felt was lonely.

We played a brisk, upbeat rendition of "Reach the Sky" to end our set. As we finished the song, the crowd let out a roar of approval.

"Thank you!" I said, beaming at the crowd as Logan came up to join me. The applause continued after we took our bows.

"Maybe we should play an encore," I murmured. There was no reply. "Logan?" I said, but when I turned in his direction, he was already making his way offstage.

HOMESICK HOTEL

Chapter 13

We spent nearly an hour after the Kingsport Auditorium show talking to audience members in the lobby. It was a whirlwind of selfies and hugs and autographing EPs. The whole thing felt like an incredible dream where I was everyone's favorite person . . . well, everyone except Logan Everett's. We pretty much ignored each other through the whole thing, even when we had to pose for pictures together.

The Hayden sisters and their mom had made it to the show, and ended up staying the entire time, talking nonstop about the concert. It turned out Zane had gotten them seats in the third row.

"It was awesome!" Corinne said, wrapping her arms around me in a bone-crushing hug.

HOMESICK HOTEL

"It was," echoed Emily as we gave them all hugs. "Thank you both again so much."

As they left, I waited for Logan to scowl at me or say something rude, but he just walked away. Clearly, he was still mad about our argument onstage. I tried not to let it get under my skin, but I couldn't help it. It wasn't like *I* had done anything wrong, but Logan was treating me like I was the one who almost ruined our show!

Once the van was loaded, we headed to a pizzeria for an early dinner and discussed the show. Well, Dad and Zane discussed it. Logan and I mainly glowered at our food and avoided eye contact with each other.

"According to my tally, we sold fifty-two EPs and just under three hundred tickets," Dad said, consulting his phone. "And we've sold a total of ninety-four EPs so far." Zane let out a low whistle.

"Not too shabby," he said, winking at me and Logan. "Of course, what really counts is how you guys felt about the show."

Logan said nothing.

"I thought it went okay," I managed.

Zane's eyebrows shot up. "Only okay?" he said. "That's a shame. I thought y'all had a rocky start, but you finished strongly. In my opinion, you both played with a lot of fire."

"Great," I said, feeling slightly relieved. Although I'd sensed that the audience had enjoyed the show, for me it was a blur of emotion. The only thing I remembered clearly was the expression on Logan's face when I'd told him he was falling apart.

I darted a glance at Logan. To my surprise, he was looking at me.

"I guess I wasn't so terrible after all," he muttered under his breath.

Frustration turned my cheeks hot. The last thing I needed was for Logan to tell Zane and Dad about our argument onstage. In their eyes, that would just be more evidence that we weren't ready to cut a record. But I couldn't say any of that out loud, so instead I shoved a breadstick in my mouth and stared at my plate.

Zane and Dad didn't seem to hear Logan's comment.

HOMESICK HOTEL

"We've got an hour before it gets dark," Zane said, checking his watch. "Anyone feel like being a tourist?"

"I'm up for it," Dad said amiably. "Tenney, what do you think?"

This morning I'd have given away my lucky guitar pick to have the chance to explore a new town. But right now, I just wanted to be alone. I shook my head.

Dad gave me a curious look. "All right then. How about you, Logan?"

Logan stared at his shoes. "No, thanks," he said. "I'm actually kind of tired."

"I'm not surprised after that great concert you two put on this afternoon," Zane said. "Maybe it's better that you two rest up. We have a big day tomorrow!"

We all nodded. Tomorrow was the last and busiest day of our tour. We were playing a show in the morning in Sevierville, then driving two hundred miles across the state to play an evening show in Thompson's Station, a pocket-sized town outside Nashville, before driving home. Every minute was going to be jam-packed.

TENNEY

As we put on our coats and scarves, my phone vibrated with a new text, and I pulled it out.

Mom had sent me a photo. It showed Waylon in his doggy reindeer antlers and red Rudolph nose, his tongue lolling in a doggy smile as he posed with Mason and Aubrey at the Howl-iday Ramble. They all looked so happy, as if they didn't miss me at all.

Sadness cut through me. Tomorrow was Christmas Eve and instead of enjoying my favorite time of the year with my family, I was going to be playing two more shows with sour, unfocused Logan. For the first time since we'd left Nashville, I really wished I wasn't on tour anymore. I just wanted to get our last two shows over with and go home.

It was snowing by the time we left the restaurant, tiny flakes that melted before they hit the ground. Logan glanced at me a couple of times as we walked through the cold, but he didn't say anything, so neither did I.

HOMESICK HOTEL

As soon as we got inside, Zane headed to the business center and Logan said he had to make a call and peeled off before anyone could say anything.

Dad and I headed back to our room. As we waited in the elevator, I leaned against him. I wished I could tell him about my argument with Logan during the show, but I didn't want to say or do anything that might jeopardize whatever chance we had left to record an album. And if I was being honest, I really didn't feel like talking to anyone right now, even Dad.

I think he sensed that, because he didn't ask me any questions. When we got to our hotel room, he opened it with the sliding key, then turned to me.

"I'm gonna go do a little exploring," he said. "You seem like you need some time alone."

"Yeah," I admitted, thankful that he knew me so well.

Dad nodded. "I know touring can be hard, Tenney," he said carefully. "It's okay if you're not having fun all the time. It's still going to make you a better performer. You just have to get through the tough times."

I nodded. I knew he was right, but that didn't make me feel any better.

After Dad left, I shut the door and I set my guitar on the bed, lying down beside it. I still felt a jumble of emotions: sad and angry, ashamed and lonely, and most of all homesick.

I glanced at the hotel window. Snowflakes hit the glass and melted into droplets of water, like miniature tears. The few cars in the parking lot were coated in dirty-looking frost, and the sky was heavy with gloomy gray clouds. The one dash of color was a red Christmas ribbon that someone had tied in a bow to a streetlight. As I watched the ribbon's loose ends flutter in the wind, the holiday song I'd been working on floated back into my mind.

I sat up, feeling a pulse of inspiration. I grabbed my songwriting journal and a pen from my backpack and took out my guitar, and curled up in a comfy soft chair by the window. I looked out at the wintry view and played my new melody, thinking about the day. My belly burned as I remembered how upset I'd gotten at Logan for his mistakes during the concert, and how smug he'd been at dinner.

HOMESICK HOTEL

He didn't seem bothered at all by the glitches that had nearly ruined our first three shows. But when we were offstage he seemed angry, as if everything I said or did was spoiling our tour. As if I was a nuisance. As if he would rather be touring without me.

I set my guitar on the floor and grabbed my journal. Ideas and images started exploding in my brain, describing all the things I'd been feeling since we started the tour. I wrote about everything: about my loneliness, and the cold of winter; about missing home and my family; and about the red ribbon on the streetlamp. I had so many thoughts, I felt like I couldn't write them down fast enough. Within minutes, I had nearly two pages of lyric ideas.

I took a deep breath. The air felt electric in my lungs, and I wanted to keep going.

I hauled my guitar back onto my lap and played what I had of my song's structure, looking at my idea brainstorm. As I did, lyrics started flowing.

Sometimes when I write a song, I end up having to twist and change words far away from my original idea to make it work musically. Not this time. The deeper I got into the song, the more quickly the music and lyrics seemed to fall into a seamless whole. It wasn't the fun, silly tune I'd imagined writing when I first thought about creating a holiday song, but somehow it was better. It was a song that made my homesickness and anger seem real and valid, and working on it had made me feel like I was closer to home.

I managed to get to the end of the song and play it through a few times before the room door clicked open and Dad poked his head in.

"How's it going?" he asked.

"Okay," I replied, stretching out my fingers.

When Dad slipped inside, I saw he was carrying a pair of paper drink cups. He set them on the hotel desk and fished a little paper bag out of his jacket.

"I got us hot chocolates and a cookie for dessert," he said, handing me a cup.

I took a sip of chocolate and pulled the cookie out of the bag, a fat little snowman gleaming with sugar. His jaunty smile made me laugh.

"Thanks, Dad," I said.

HOMESICK HOTEL

He kissed my head and hung an arm around me in a hug. "You seem to be feeling a little better," he said.

"I am," I said, taking another sip. And as warmth seeped through me, I realized I really meant it.

FALLING APART

Chapter 14

I awoke the next morning to Dad gently sweeping the hair from my face. It was pitch-black and chilly, and it still felt like the middle of the night.

I peeked one eye open and looked at the clock. "Six thirty?" I asked. "Too early."

"Come on, kiddo. Rise and shine," Dad said softly, flipping on the lamp next to my bed. "Let's get moving. We've got a big day ahead. You'll have plenty of time to sleep in your own bed when we get home tonight."

Home tonight! The best two words I'd heard all week. I jumped out of bed and showered and dressed quickly, trying to ignore the damp draft seeping through the hotel windows. It was only slightly warmer in the lobby when we brought down our suitcases to check out. Outside, the sky was a bitter gray

FALLING APART

swirl, and the wind was sharp, but we didn't let it slow us down. We grabbed doughnuts at a coffee shop and by seven thirty, we were heading south on I-81.

"Last day of the tour!" Zane announced with a grin. "How's everybody feeling?"

I peered at Logan. He was staring down at his phone as usual.

"Good," I replied, speaking for both of us. "I'm great actually."

Logan avoided my gaze. "How far is it to Sevierville?" he asked.

"A little under ninety miles," Zane said. "But y'all don't go on until ten thirty. We should be there way before sound check." He glanced at me in the rearview mirror and gave me a wink.

"Then once it's done, we pack up and get all the way back to Thompson's Station for the seven o'clock show," Dad said.

"And then we head home," I finished, my voice lilting up in enthusiasm.

"Yup," Zane confirmed. "If we do this right, we'll be back in Nashville by ten o'clock this evening, just in time for Christmas."

I nodded. Tonight, I would get to kiss my mom good night, and sleep in my own bed with Waylon at my feet, and wake up for Christmas with my family. The idea made me so happy, I gave myself a little hug.

"Y'all just need to play two phenomenal shows first," Zane said with a smile.

"Easy as pie," Dad echoed.

I felt like a bubble had just popped. I'd been so immersed in my daydream of being home, I'd stopped thinking about how important these last two shows were. If Logan and I fell apart onstage, there was no way Zane would think we were ready to record an album.

Both shows have to be fantastic, I thought, glancing at Logan. He was slouched in the seat beside me, wearing headphones and a glum expression. Although part of me was still frustrated over our argument yesterday, I knew that I had to break the ice between us before we started our next show or else our performance would be doomed.

Impulsively, I tapped Logan on the shoulder.

"Yeah?" he said curtly, looking at me.

"These shows are going to be fun," I told him as

persuasively as I could muster. "Let's make them count."

He blinked, and I pasted on a wide smile, trying to convince him—and myself—that I wanted to mend fences.

"Uh-huh," Logan grunted, like he was agreeing to take out the garbage, and turned to the window.

I stared at my feet, a lump of angry hurt rising in my throat. I'd tried to be nice and once again, Logan had brushed me off. It took every ounce of my being not to say something sharp to him in that moment, but I held off. The last thing we needed was for Dad and Zane to see us fighting any more than we already were.

I rested my forehead against the window's cool glass, trying to calm down. *Forget Logan*, I told myself. *I'll just have to do everything I can to make our next two shows great.*

The sky looked like a stormy sea the whole way to Sevierville, a pretty pint-sized town near the edges of the Smoky Mountains where Dolly Parton grew up. I'd never been there, but as we drove up the main street, it felt cozy and familiar. Clusters of shoppers

passed in and out of festively decorated storefronts.
Thousands of twinkle lights lined every eave and
window. The lights hung in wide looped garlands
across the intersections and wrapped around the
trees along the road. It felt like the town was glowing
with joy under the dark winter clouds.

"Wow," I breathed. "What is this?"

"Winterfest," Dad said. "Sevierville does this
every year for the holidays."

"So cool," Logan said wonderingly.

In that moment, his gaze caught mine. To my
surprise, Logan didn't scowl or turn away. He just
looked sad, and that made me sad. I wanted to talk to
him, but not in front of Dad and Zane.

When we pulled up to Sevier Middle School, the
parking lot was nearly full. Groups of kids and parents were making their way inside.

"There's your audience," Zane said, grinning
over his shoulder at me and Logan.

We parked behind the school auditorium. A
round man in a Santa hat met us outside and intro-
duced himself as the concert organizer. He grabbed a
walkie-talkie from his belt and called out a few

stagehands to help unload our gear, and then escorted us inside. As Dad and Zane set up our instruments, Logan and I followed the man in the Santa hat through cement hallways to a classroom, where he left us to warm up. But when the door closed, Logan turned to me with the same sad expression he'd had in the van.

"What is going on with you?" he asked quietly.

"With *me*?!" I said, surprised. "You're the one acting like you don't want to be here."

Logan clenched his jaw, but he didn't deny it. "Maybe if you weren't acting so crazy, I would—"

"How am I acting crazy?" I interrupted, outrage turning my voice into a squeak.

"Yesterday you yelled at me during a show to get it together," he said, "and now you're acting like that never happened."

"I was trying to be *nice* to you because I don't want you to fall apart onstage again!" Logan winced, but I kept going. "We have to be awesome! We can't bomb another show or else Zane will—" I hesitated.

"Or else Zane will what?" Logan said, looking confused.

TENNEY

I took a deep breath. "I overheard Zane and Dad talking about us," I explained. "They've been noticing that we're not getting along. And Zane basically said if the rest of our tour performances weren't great, then we probably weren't ready to cut an album."

Alarm sparked in Logan's eyes. "He said that?" he said. "Why didn't you tell me?"

"I've been trying to," I countered. "But you always had your headphones on, or were staring at your phone like the last thing you wanted to do was talk to me. I didn't want to give you one more reason to be in a bad mood."

"So instead you kept crucial information about our musical future to yourself," he said, folding his arms across his chest.

As soon as Logan said it, I realized how wrong I'd been. Of course I should have told him. Logan had worked just as hard for our musical success as I had. It was silly to think he would somehow care any less about it.

But before I could say anything else, Dad knocked on the door and poked his head in.

"Showtime!" Dad said.

FALLING APART

I darted a glance at Logan. He looked miserable, but grabbed his drumsticks and jumped up.

We didn't say anything to each other as we followed my dad down the hall and up a short flight of stairs to the stage. The thin curtain was closed, but through it, I could hear the excited babble of kids' voices.

Logan slipped behind his kit, pulling his drumsticks out of his back pocket, while I slung on my guitar and moved to my double microphone stand. We each did our own quiet adjustments, getting ready to play, until light clapping from the audience got my attention. On the other side of the curtain, the concert organizer began speaking.

"Welcome, everyone!" he said. "Thank you! We're delighted that you're here to celebrate the joy of the season through music with us today."

As he continued, I glanced over my shoulder at Logan. He was sitting ramrod straight behind his kit, drumsticks poised to play. He refused to look at me.

I took a big breath, preparing myself. *Maybe I should just perform as if Logan isn't here*, I thought to myself. But I knew I couldn't make it through a show like that. We were a team. There was no way we would be great without each other. But right now, I felt like a mountain stood between us.

Deep in my heart, I knew that this show was going to be a disaster—and there was nothing I could do about it.

TAKEN BY SURPRISE

Chapter 15

*T*he curtain opened, revealing a school gymnasium filled with junior high schoolers sitting in long rows that stretched nearly to the back of the room, where some adults stood. When they saw us, a cheer rippled through the room.

Zane and Dad stood next to the stage, whooping and whistling along with the crowd. I smiled, but my stomach churned. I hated the thought of disappointing our fans—and proving to Zane that Logan and I weren't ready to make an album after all.

Nervously, I counted us off. "Five, six, seven, eight . . ."

We dove into a bright, twangy version of "Joy to the World." Our intro started out strong, my guitar strumming perfectly in sync with Logan's driving tempo. I sang the first few lines before Logan started in on the harmony, our voices joining together perfectly. I kept waiting for Logan's rhythm to speed up, or for our vocals to go off-key. But as we reached the end of the first chorus, I could hardly believe my ears—we sounded better than ever. Soon people were tapping their feet and clapping along. When we ended the song, the audience erupted in applause.

I smiled and looked back at Logan. He was grinning at the crowd. When our eyes met, he gave me a look that said, "Let's keep going."

From there we jumped right into our next song, and then the next. We kept up a brisk pace, never pausing too long between numbers. By the time Logan stood up from his drum kit a few songs later, most of the audience was on their feet.

"Thank you," I told them as Logan swiped his guitar from its stand and moved to a microphone downstage, checking his tunings.

I stepped back, inhaling deeply. As I did, Logan threw me a nod, letting me know he was ready.

"You may not know that Logan's so talented, he plays drums *and* guitar," I told the audience.

TAKEN BY SURPRISE

"And Tenney's so talented, she plays guitar *and* banjo *and* writes most of our songs," Logan added.

I felt my cheeks go pink. "This one's called 'Reach the Sky,'" I said. The crowd jumped to their feet and cheered, and I nearly fell over in surprise.

Logan leaned over. "I guess they know this one," he whispered as our chords weaved together to form the intricate beginning of the song.

I started singing the first verse, and was surprised to hear several audience members singing along. By the time Logan and I started harmonizing on the chorus, more voices had joined in.

Suddenly, a memory flashed in my mind: watching Belle's concert and wondering whether my music would ever connect with an audience the way hers did.

I looked out at the crowd, watching them sing *my* lyrics, feeling every word: *"Gonna be myself, nobody else. Gonna reach the sky if I only try."* Hearing them sing sent my heart soaring.

TENNEY

I floated through the next hour, posing for photos, signing EPs, and talking until my throat went dry. More than one person asked when we were going to record our first "real" album, which was totally exhilarating. By the time Zane came up and told us we needed to go, I realized I was exhausted.

As we made our way through the hallways back toward the parking lot, Dad told us he had good news. "We sold out of EPs!" he said, his eyes sparkling.

Logan's jaw dropped open. "That's impossible!" he said.

"Nope, that's Tenney and Logan!" Zane said, clapping his hands on both our shoulders with an exhilarated whoop. "One hundred fifty copies, my friends! You two are on! Your! Way!"

When we reached the parking lot, I noticed that the clouds had gotten darker, and that the wind had started gusting. My breath froze in the air as we made our way to the van. It felt like my cheeks were being blasted by icy crystals.

Once we were inside and shut the doors against

the cold, Logan and I looked at each other. We had just played the show of our lives, but we both knew that we still had unsettled business between us. We didn't really have time to dwell on that, though. We still had one more show to play today, and I didn't want to ruin the optimism I knew we were both feeling right now. As I settled back into my seat and stared out the front windshield, I felt like I could do anything.

Zane pulled onto a country road, heading east toward Thompson's Station. "Storm's coming up faster than I thought," he murmured, squinting at the sky.

Dad gave a grim nod.

I pressed my forehead to the window. Although it was still afternoon, the sky was dark with muddy storm clouds, the sky bruised dark blue around it.

After a few minutes on the two-lane road, it started sleeting, slushy drops that hit the van's windows in bursts. A strong gale pummeled the van, and I gasped.

"You okay, Tenney?" Dad said.

I nodded, forcing myself to be calm.

"Don't worry," Dad said reassuringly.

I looked out the windshield. Ahead of us, the road stretched like a narrow gray river without end. We pushed onward. After about twenty minutes, the sleet thickened into snow. The wind was louder now, and I could hear the low rumble of thunder in the distance.

"The drive might take longer than we thought," Zane said, not taking his eyes off the road.

"That's okay. Safety first," Dad said, sounding tense.

After another fifteen minutes, it was snowing so hard that we slowed to a crawl. The road grew slushier and visibility got even worse. That's when the van started making noises. Well, one noise, really: a wheezing sound that started as we climbed uphill, like the van was protesting having to move.

"Sounds like the engine," Dad said.

"I know," Zane replied grimly.

Suddenly, the engine started making an awful grinding noise and the whole van began trembling.

"What's happening?!" I said, fear sending my voice into a squeak.

TAKEN BY SURPRISE

"Pull over there," Dad told Zane, gesturing to a shoulder just ahead. Zane drove us onto the shoulder and turned off the van. The grinding stopped and the lights turned off, leaving us in silent darkness.

"Do me a favor," Zane said to Dad. "Check your GPS, see where we are."

Dad clicked around on his phone and waited. "No service," he said, shaking his head. They tried Zane's phone, too, but it had the same problem.

After a second, Dad flipped on the interior light above us. He looked back at me and Logan, his forehead creased with worry.

"Tenney, is your phone working?" he asked.

I checked it. At the top of my home screen, above the photo of me and Waylon, there were no bars.

"I don't think so," I said, but I handed Dad my phone anyway.

"What about you, Logan?" Zane asked.

Logan shook his head.

I squinted out the window. Snow was coming down hard, and I couldn't see much beyond dark trees and driving whiteness.

★ ★

TENNEY

"So much for calling a tow truck," Dad muttered. As a look passed between him and Zane, my stomach sank in dread.

We were stranded in a horrible snowstorm with no phone service. Were we going to end up trapped here overnight?

STRANDED

Chapter 16

*I*nside the van, all was quiet except for the constant, shifting sweep of the snowy wind outside. Fresh snowflakes quickly covered the glass in a frosty layer, but I could still make out the narrow, wet country road outside. I couldn't see any other cars. We were all alone.

"What do you want to do?" Zane asked Dad after they'd both spent a few minutes trying and failing to make phone calls.

Dad frowned at the falling snow outside. "There was a sign a few miles back for a service station and a hotel," he observed. "We can't be too far from it. So one of us stays here with Tenney and Logan, and the other starts walking till they can flag someone down."

"I can go," Zane offered, but Dad shook his head.

"I've got winter boots on. I'll go," he said.

Fear chilled me down to my toes. "Dad, the storm's really bad," I protested. "I don't want you to go."

"Sweetheart, we don't have a choice," Dad said quietly. "We need help."

"I know," I whispered, trying to ignore the tornado of worry whirling inside me.

"It'll be fine, I promise," Dad told me, squeezing my shoulder.

"There's a flashlight and an emergency kit in the back," Zane said. He turned to Logan and me. "You two hang tight. I'm going to stay outside to flag down any passing cars."

Dad and Zane got out of the van, leaving Logan and me in the backseat. After a few moments, Dad reappeared, wearing a hooded reflective jacket over his winter coat and holding a big flashlight. He turned it on and waved it around, but with all the snow coming down, its light seemed pale and weak.

"Be back soon!" Dad shouted through the window.

I nodded, but as he disappeared out into the

storm, my breath flooded out in a shudder, and I struggled not to burst into tears.

"He'll be okay," Logan said firmly, like it was the only thing in the world he knew for sure.

"You don't know that," I said.

We sat in silence, listening to the falling snow and ice tap against the sides of the van. I peered out the windshield. Zane stood in front of the van, watching for approaching cars as the headlights' bright beams illuminated the snow swirling around him.

I shivered, closing my eyes. All I could think about was my dad trudging through freezing snow and darkness along the deserted country road, looking for someone to help us. I took a deep breath, trying to calm myself.

Logan sniffled and I looked over. In the half-light, I could see wet streaks on Logan's cheeks.

I was so surprised that I didn't know what to say for a moment.

"Are you okay?" I said at last.

"Not really," Logan said. He gave me a miserable look.

TENNEY

"My dad's going to get help, and we'll be back on the road in no time," I tried to reassure him, even though I was scared, too. "And you heard Zane; we just played a great show and sold out all of our EPs. That means we can make our album and—"

"That's not what's bothering me, Tenney!" Logan blurted.

I drew back. "Then . . . what's going on?"

"The last few days have just been really hard," he confessed.

"I understand," I said. "I've been super home-sick, too."

"But you *don't* understand," Logan said. "My little brother has been calling and texting me every day, asking when I'm coming home. I remember doing the same thing while my dad was on tour when I was Jude's age. But my dad was gone so often that after a while, I figured that being on the road must be really cool."

I nodded sympathetically, remembering how glamorous I had assumed life on tour would be.

"And so I thought that *our* tour was going to be this amazing experience," Logan continued, looking out the window. "But when things began falling apart, starting with our first show, I realized that being on tour is really hard. It's not the exciting life that I imagined my dad has been living all this time. He missed out on so many things that were important to me because he's always on tour. So why would he choose *this* over being home with me and Jude?" Logan sniffled and wiped his face. "Did he just not want to be with us?"

My heart ached for Logan, but I didn't know how to comfort him.

After a moment of silence, I finally asked, "Why didn't you talk to me about this sooner?"

Logan looked a little embarrassed. "I tried to after the Franklin show," he said. "I came by your hotel room to talk, but you were on the phone. Then when we were playing around in the lobby in Knoxville, I almost told you, but I didn't think you would understand how I was feeling. You've been acting so upbeat all the time, doing everything you can to make the tour great."

"I was just doing that so I wouldn't think about what I was missing at home," I admitted.

TENNEY

Logan nodded, understanding filling his eyes. "This whole time I've been thinking that our tour was falling apart because our shows had technical problems. But after we played that great show this afternoon, I realized that the only thing that was getting in the way of us having a great tour . . . was me."

I shook my head, feeling my heart swell up with sympathy for Logan.

"Don't say that," I said. "This whole time, we've been sad about our families, and being away from home. We just reacted to it in different ways."

He nodded, but I could tell that he didn't feel any better.

"I wish we had talked to each other about how we were feeling," I said.

"You mean before we got stuck in a snowstorm?" Logan asked with a bleak laugh.

We shared a sad smile, and I looked out the window. I couldn't see anything beyond the snow anymore.

"Every tour is different," I tried to reassure him. "I'm sure our next one will be way better."

"Maybe," he said. Then he paused, looking up at me. "But I'm not sure I want to find out."

I drew in a breath. "What are you saying?" I asked him.

Logan opened his mouth to speak, but suddenly, we heard a loud *HONNNNK!!*

Bright lights swept over us, blinding me for a moment. When my eyes adjusted, I saw Zane waving his arms back and forth as a hulking tow truck with snow tires pulled in front of the van. After a moment, the truck's passenger door opened and Dad hopped out.

"Dad!" I exclaimed.

The next few minutes were a blur of piling into the snow and staying out of the way as the adults hitched the van to the tow truck. At one point, I glanced at Logan. He stood watching the van get hoisted onto the tow truck's platform, but I could tell that he was still thinking about our conversation. I wanted to go talk to him, but not in front of Dad and Zane.

We crowded into the truck's cab with the driver. As the powerful rumble of the engine started under us, I sat back under my dad's arm, relieved to be safe.

TENNEY

"We'll be back on the road in no time," Dad said, squeezing me in. "We've got plenty of time to get you to your last show."

I nodded and peered at Logan as he gazed out the window in silence. What did Logan mean when he said that he wasn't sure he wanted to go on tour again? Was this the end of the road for us?

I have to make this final show count, I told myself. *It's my last opportunity to show Logan that this tour was worth it.*

TO THE RESCUE

Chapter 17

*I*t took half an hour to drive through the storm to the nearest garage, but only five minutes for the mechanic to figure out what was wrong with the van.

"Your engine overheated," he said to Zane, wiping the grease off his hands with a towel. I noticed that he wore a patch on his coveralls that read HELLO, MY NAME IS VERNON! "You need a new radiator."

"Sounds simple enough," Zane said. "How long will that take? We've got a show in Thompson's Station at seven o'clock."

"Seven o'clock *tonight*? In Thompson's Station?" Vernon chuckled sadly, patting Zane on the shoulder as if he'd just said we needed to be in Hawaii in an hour. "Not gonna happen."

"But it's the last show of our tour," I blurted.

"Sorry," Vernon told me. "It's almost four, and

you've got two other cars ahead of you. Even if I *could* magically fix the radiator, there's an accident ten miles up on I-40 so they just closed it indefinitely due to the storm. Hopefully, it'll be open by tomorrow."

"Tomorrow?" I echoed, my thoughts going into a tailspin. "But tomorrow's Christmas. We're supposed to be home tonight."

Dad sighed. "It looks like that's not going to happen, honey."

"Yeah," Zane said. "We're going to have to cancel the Thompson's Station show and find a motel."

I leaned against a wall. I felt dizzy, like I'd just stepped off an amusement park ride. Everything that had given me hope for the end of our tour—playing one last great show and being home on Christmas Eve—had suddenly blown away like a snowflake in the cold winter air.

Vernon drove us to the nearest hotel off the interstate, a lean single-story building with green shutters and a red roof covered in snow. The parking

TO THE RESCUE

lot was crowded with cars and a charter bus outside, and the lobby was crammed with travelers shaking snow off their hats and coats.

"We need two rooms for tonight," Zane told the lady behind the reception desk after we'd made our way through the crowd.

"You're in luck," she replied. "You got my last two rooms." She started talking about room rates with Zane and Dad.

"I need to call my mom," Logan told me. He stepped away, pulling out his phone, and moved across the lobby.

I just stood there as travelers jostled by me, still hardly believing that this was happening.

"Honey, this might take a while, so why don't you sit down?" Dad suggested. "I'll come get you when we're checked in."

The only empty chair in the lobby was right by the entrance. I sat down, huddling into my coat. Every now and then the automatic door *whooshed* open and I'd get hit with a cold blast of wintry air, as if to remind me that this was real life.

The doors *whooshed* open again and an elderly

couple walked in. "If the snow keeps up at this rate, we might be spending Christmas night here, too," the woman said to her husband.

Before I could process that thought, my phone buzzed with a new text, and I pulled it out. When we were out in the storm, my phone hadn't gotten any reception. Now that we were at the hotel, I was receiving the messages I'd been sent in the past few hours. They were all from Jaya.

> 3:14 p.m.   *Happy last day of your awesome tour!*
> 3:16 p.m.   *It's snowing like crazy here in Nashville!*
> 3:17 p.m.   *I'm so excited to see you tomorrow at the holiday jam!!*
> 3:21 p.m.   *Can't wait to hear all the details about your adventure!*
> 3:40 p.m.   *Everything okay?*

Reading Jaya's texts made my heart hurt. I texted back, telling Jaya all about getting stranded and rescued. It only took her a few seconds to reply.

TO THE RESCUE

That's crazy! I'm so glad you are all right.

Just a moment later, she sent another text: *Will you be home for Christmas?*

Her question made a hard lump rise in my throat.

I don't know, I wrote back. *I hope so.*

I looked at the sparse Christmas decorations scattered around the lobby. Across from me, the hotel diner bustled with stranded travelers, who squinted miserably out the windows at the snow. Far in the back, a lonely stool was perched on a sad, dusty corner stage with a sign that said MERRY CHRISTMAS!

My heart sank. I didn't want to spend Christmas here. I wanted to be home with my family. I stared at my boots, tears welling in my eyes as the doors *whooshed* open and closed beside me. Suddenly, I couldn't stand to be in the lobby a moment longer.

I slipped outside. Snow was coming down in sheets. I pulled my scarf up around my mouth and stepped forward, tilting my face to the dark sky. As the prickly chill of snowflakes hit my skin, I let myself cry at last. My tears mixed with falling snow, forming a melty slush on my cheeks. I gulped down a deep breath of chilly air. Its sharpness sliced through my lungs, but it made me feel better.

Just then, I spotted Logan through the door. His phone was pressed to his ear, and I could tell he was upset.

My heart panged—was he telling Jude that he wouldn't be coming home tonight?

As I thought of all the things Logan had told me in the car, I suddenly realized how much harder this must be for him. Of course I was sad that I wouldn't be home for Christmas Eve, but at least I had my dad here. Logan's dad was an entire ocean away, and the rest of his family was all the way across Tennessee.

And even though I had missed out on a bunch of my favorite holiday traditions over the past few days, I never questioned whether our tour was worthwhile. But now Logan seemed to be questioning his entire musical future.

Logan hung up his phone and quickly wiped his eyes before joining Zane by the elevator. As Logan disappeared behind the elevator doors, I realized that I had to do *something* to help him.

TO THE RESCUE

But what *could* I do?

I had no control over the storm, or the snow, or the roads. There wasn't anything I could do to make Logan feel better about his dad or to get us home tonight. And now that our last show had been canceled, I'd lost my chance to prove to Logan that our tour had been worthwhile—or had I?

Suddenly, I had an idea. I stepped back into the lobby and kicked the snow off my boots, my gaze drifting to the tiny stage at the back of the hotel restaurant. What if we had the last show of our tour right here in the hotel?

Dad ran over to me. "There you are, Tenney! You okay?" he asked, gently swiping a strand of hair out of my eyes.

"I'm okay," I said. "But I need you to help me with something."

ONE LAST SHOW

Chapter 18

J told Dad my idea. "We have the stage, the equipment, and the audience," I said. "Now we just need a little holiday spirit."

Dad seemed surprised that I wanted to do *anything* after our disastrous travel day, but he was supportive. "Good music might help take people's minds off being stranded," Dad mused. "Let me go see who I can find to talk to about this."

He went up to the reception desk and brought over the hotel manager, a petite, businesslike woman named Diana. She loved my idea, and when she checked with the diner's manager, he loved it, too.

Dad turned to me and grinned. "Looks like we've got a show to put on. Do you want to go get Logan and Zane?"

ONE LAST SHOW

I shook my head with a wry smile. "Let's make it a surprise."

Dad raised his eyebrows. "Whatever you say," he replied.

Dad and I swung into action. The stage in the diner was too small for Logan's drum kit, so we brought out Logan's guitar and set up a second stool for an acoustic show. Then we tuned the guitars, plugged them into our amplifiers, and tested the sound and the microphones.

"Shall I go get Logan and Zane?" Dad asked once we were done setting up.

I grinned and nodded.

I was excited to perform, but as I waited for Dad to come back, I realized how crowded and loud the space was. Two harried waitresses were running between tables, and the patrons seemed grumpy.

"Watch it!" hissed an older man as I swung my guitar around and nearly hit him.

"I'm sorry," I said.

He scowled and sat down at a nearby booth in a huff, his back to me.

TENNEY

Maybe this was a bad idea, I thought as I sat down on the stool. If this show turned out to be a bust, Logan would never forgive me for ruining the end of our already disastrous tour.

At that moment, Logan and Zane appeared in the doorway. Our eyes locked.

"Tenney?" Logan said. "What are—"

"Excuse me, everyone," I said into my microphone. "Happy holidays!"

The diner was a swarming sea of people eating, drinking, and talking over each other. Only a couple of people seemed to notice me. Logan looked around dubiously.

I swallowed hard, but pressed on. "I know that most of you are sad to be away from your families this Christmas Eve," I started. A few more people looked up from their plates, so I continued. "But since we're all stuck here, why not celebrate the spirit of the season together?"

By now, a lot more people were listening and a few diners even hushed the remaining talkers.

I took a deep breath and looked at Logan. "Christmas is a time to show people how much we care about them," I said. "And so tonight, I want to play a new song for a friend as a reminder that he's not alone."

Logan crossed his arms warily, but his expression softened.

Settling my hands on my guitar, I began to play. My fingers danced over the strings as the gentle, silvery melody of my song rang out from my guitar. As I let myself get caught up in the music, any worries I had about whether the show would work out melted away. I was playing for Logan, for the end of our tour, for my hope that we would be home tomorrow.

I leaned into my microphone and started to sing.

It's an icy, bitter night
On a long and lonely road
We've been driving now for hours
Maybe we'll never get back home
My heart is frozen hard from sadness
You're the flip side of good cheer
We're many miles away from family
The season's joys feel nowhere near.

TENNEY

I looked up from my guitar. Logan looked as if he was on the verge of tears as I jumped into the chorus.

When you hear this song,
I hope you think of me
When you sing this song
Let your heart fly free
May that be this season's gift to you from me.

As the song continued, the diner patrons listened attentively, hanging on every word. Confident and relieved, I poured my heart into the bridge, strumming quietly at the beginning, getting louder with every word as I built up to the final verse.

All around us the storm is raging
But we can win the fight we're facing
We're tied together by a ribbon of hope
We can go on
If we stay strong.
'Cause when the skies finally clear
We'll stop feeling so alone

ONE LAST SHOW

All our dreams will reappear
And together we'll find home.

Logan smiled at the last line. And at that
moment, I knew that even though I couldn't fix
everything that had gone wrong, I had at least made
his Christmas Eve a little brighter.

Wrapping up the final notes of the song, I finished with a flourish and everyone cheered.

"Thank you," I said into the microphone, eyeing
Logan nervously. I couldn't be sure that he would join
me onstage, but I had to try. "And now I'd like to
invite up to the stage my very talented partner, Logan
Everett."

Logan's mouth narrowed into a small, surprised
O. He hesitated for a split second, but then
approached the stage and grabbed his guitar as the
audience applauded politely.

I leaned over to him. "You ready?"

"I'm not sure," he said. "Ready for what?"

"The last show of our tour?" I said. It came out
like a question, but I gave him a confident smile.

Logan looked around at the diner patrons who

were waiting patiently for our next song. For a
moment, I was worried that he would bolt offstage.
But then he cracked a grin, and I knew his answer
was yes.

The next half hour was full of music—boppy and
beautiful, simple and soulful. We sailed from a ballad
to a Christmas carol, on to a hard-driving country-
rock tune and then into a melancholy duet. After
each song, the applause got louder.

As we neared the end of the set, we played
Portia's holiday tune, "Cold Creek Christmas." So
many voices joined us as we sang. I had no idea
so many people knew that song.

"May your season sing with joy," Logan and I sang
in harmony. *"May this music always stay with you."*

As our voices rang out, I looked around the
room, gazing at the circle of warm faces. Although I
didn't know anyone's name, I felt as if we were surrounded by friends. Just over an hour ago I'd been
in tears, desperately wishing I could go home. But in
this moment, with music flowing through me, there
was no place on earth I'd rather be.

A CHRISTMAS SURPRISE

Chapter 19

*T*he whole world was bright when I opened my eyes the next morning. I bounced out of bed and raced to the nearest window to look out. Thick snow blanketed the parking lot below, but the sky above it was a dazzling, clear blue. Seeing the view, I was filled with hope. The storm was over. Maybe we could get home today.

"Merry Christmas!" I said.

Dad grinned over his newspaper. "Look who's finally out of hibernation!" he teased with a wink. "Although I guess you're entitled to sleep in. You did play a pretty killer show."

"I thought so!" I chirped, giving Dad a cheeky smile.

He laughed. "I'm proud of you, sweetheart," Dad said. "You took a bad situation and turned it around.

TENNEY

You and Logan really helped people find their holiday spirit, I could tell."

"I actually think it helped Logan and me more than anybody," I said thoughtfully.

"How's that?" Dad asked.

I paused, sorting through my emotions and thoughts. "I feel like I spent so much time during our tour getting upset when things didn't turn out how I expected," I finally replied. "But looking back now, those challenges helped us, in a way. Like the storm. If it hadn't happened, Logan might have—" I paused.

I suddenly realized that even though we played a great show last night, I still didn't know how Logan was feeling about our tour—or about the future of our duo. Could this have been our last show?

"Logan might have what, sweetie?" Dad said, looking confused.

"Um, nothing," I said quickly, not wanting to get into it. "My point is, everything that happened yesterday made me realize that I have so much to be grateful for."

A CHRISTMAS SURPRISE

"I'm glad you feel that way," Dad said.

"Me, too," I said.

Dad looked out the window and sighed. "Now we just have to see if the roads are dug out and if the van's ready."

"Right," I breathed, worry creeping up on me again. The mechanic had been swamped with cars yesterday. He might not have had a chance to fix our van yet, and if he hadn't, well, we probably weren't getting home for Christmas.

Dad's phone buzzed with a text and he checked it.

"Zane wants us downstairs in a half hour so we can head over to the garage ASAP," he said.

While I scrambled to get dressed, Dad threw everything into our suitcases. We hustled downstairs to the lobby, where Zane and Logan were waiting.

"Merry Christmas," I said to them.

"Merry Christmas to you," Zane replied, tipping forward his porkpie hat.

Just then, Diana the hotel manager popped her head into the lobby from the doorway leading to the diner.

"Great! Y'all haven't left yet," she said, speeding into the room. She carried a full tray of hot drink cups and a pillowy bakery bag.

"What's all this?" Zane asked in surprise.

"Breakfast for the road," Diana said, handing the drink tray to Zane and the bag to me. "We've got hot chocolates and coffees, and in the bag, there's muffins and egg sandwiches."

"Wow, thank you so much," I said.

"No, thank *you*, all of you," Diana replied. "People were so sad and stressed out last night, and you helped change that. Now, when they think about the Christmas Eve snowstorm, they'll remember you and your music. I know that's what I'll remember."

I hugged her and she squeezed me back.

"Y'all are really something special," she said, looking at Logan and me. "I can't wait to hear more of your music!"

I thanked her and looked tentatively at Logan. He nodded, but I couldn't tell if he was trying to reassure me or if he was just being polite.

The hotel shuttle waited for us outside. The

A CHRISTMAS SURPRISE

mechanic's garage was just a few blocks away. Although the streets had been cleared, icy slushy piles of snow were still everywhere. We turned into the garage parking lot. A few people stood outside, their breath billowing in frozen clouds as they chatted in front of a red SUV with its hood up.

"Do you see the van?" I whispered. Logan shook his head, frowning.

Vernon stepped out from behind the SUV as we lugged our bags off the shuttle.

"Y'all are up early," he said, raising an eyebrow.

"Well . . . it's Christmas," Dad pointed out a bit awkwardly.

"Oh, yeah," Vernon deadpanned, wiping his hands on his jumpsuit. "I've been working so hard, I clean forgot."

My heart sank. *I bet he hasn't even gotten to our van yet*, I thought.

But then a tiny smile curled onto Vernon's face. "Your present's over there," he said, gesturing across the lot. I looked over and spotted the van, shining in the sun.

"It's fixed?!" I yelped.

"That's right," he smiled, looking from me to Logan. "A little birdie at the hotel let me know about the show y'all put on last night. It got me thinking that maybe I ought to do my own good deed for Christmas and get up extra early today."

He turned to Zane and Dad, handing them the keys. "The new radiator's all installed and she's working well," he said.

I squealed and Logan covered his ears.

Everyone laughed.

After Zane paid, he shook the mechanic's hand. "Thank you, friend," he said.

"You're welcome," Vernon said. He nodded toward the highway. "I hear the roads are clear, so y'all should have a straight shot home. Safe travels and Merry Christmas."

As we pulled out of the parking lot, I took a frothy sip of hot chocolate and felt myself relax. Outside, the blue sky rolled by above glistening snow-covered fields and wooden fences strung with red-ribbon garlands.

Zane peered at us in the rearview mirror. "I was

very impressed with you two last night—and during the rest of this tour, as a matter of fact," he said. "I know it wasn't always easy, but y'all had some great performances."

"Well, except for that one show where the audio stopped working," I said.

"Or the one where we showed up to a room full of tiny choir singers!" Dad added lightly.

"Or the one that we didn't get to play in Thompson's Station!" Logan chimed in.

We all started laughing. It felt good to be able to look back on the tour's less-than-perfect moments with a smile.

"You win some, you lose some," Zane said amiably. "No matter what, this tour was an achievement you two should be proud of."

I smiled, but couldn't bear to look at Logan. Our show last night had been one of the best we'd ever played, but what if it wasn't enough to convince him to keep Tenney & Logan going?

"So now I'd say it's about time that we put together a real record," Zane continued. "Whaddya think of that?"

TENNEY

"Yes!" I blurted, my heart fluttering. But then I dared a glance at Logan.

He stared out the window for a moment. "Actually . . ." he started. My heart dropped to my stomach.

Then Logan looked at me and smiled. "I think the first track we record should be Tenney's new song," he replied.

He put his fist out, and I gave it a bump, my heart soaring.

Zane turned a knob on the radio, and Belle Starr's voice rang out from the van's speakers.

You can be a star like me
Know who you are and you'll be free
Be proud of yourself and love what you see
That's when you'll see who you can be!

I smiled, thinking of how far we had come since we opened for Belle just two months ago. Touring was definitely one of the toughest things I'd ever done, but I was so proud that we'd ended on a high note.

A CHRISTMAS SURPRISE

That's when I realized that maybe Belle's touring superstition made sense—after all, our first show in Franklin *had* set the tone for the rest of our disastrous tour. But last night's show was the one I would hold in my heart forever.

THE ROAD HOME

Chapter 20

*I*t took us over three hours to get home because of traffic and wet roads, but somehow, I didn't mind. Knowing that Logan would be reunited with his mom and Jude, and that Dad and I would get to see our family soon, kept me alive with anticipation. When the Nashville skyline finally emerged in the smoky distance, I couldn't help grinning.

"Music City, USA!" Zane shouted. And as we drove past a WELCOME TO NASHVILLE! sign, we all cheered. It felt as if we'd been gone for months, rather than just a few days.

Our first stop was Logan's house. When we rolled up to the white cottage, Zane and Dad got out to unload Logan's drums and guitar. Logan gathered his coat and backpack and then paused.

THE ROAD HOME

"Now that the tour's over, I guess we won't be rehearsing together as often," he said.

"I guess not," I replied. A wave of sadness washed over me. The tour had been so tough, but now that it was over, part of me wished it wasn't. "Maybe we should just get back on the road and start another tour?" I joked.

"No way," he said, offering a crooked smile. "But maybe someday."

My eyes lit up. "I'm really glad to hear you say that," I told him.

Logan nodded and looked out the window at his house. "Touring was really hard," he admitted, "but looking back, I can see that there were a lot of great moments that made it all worth it. And now that we've been through it, I think I understand my dad better—and maybe even feel a little closer to him." He turned and looked me in the eye. "I'm not sure I would have realized that if it weren't for you. So thank you, Tenney."

He stuck out his hand for me to shake. I looked at him dubiously, and pulled him in for a hug. He let out a surprised "oof!" Then he hugged me back, just as hard.

Finally, he slid open the van door and hopped out.

As the van started pulling away, I watched Logan open the door and sweep up his little brother in a long-awaited embrace.

It took eight minutes to get from Logan's house to mine, but every second felt like forever. The moment the van rolled to a stop, I threw open the door and raced up to our porch.

The front door opened before I even got up the steps. Mom and Aubrey stood there, with Mason behind them. Seeing me, Aubrey shrieked and started hopping up and down and suddenly I was in Mom's arms, hugging her and trying not to cry, and Waylon was barking and jumping and licking the side of my face until I hugged him, too.

After spending a few minutes getting settled in, we gathered in the living room to open presents.

THE ROAD HOME

"My concertina!" Aubrey shrieked, tearing away the wrapping paper and holding the miniature accordion to her heart.

I smiled, flipping the pages of my brand-new songwriting journal.

"Maybe you can play it for your holiday jam duet with Mom," I suggested as Aubrey fiddled with the concertina's buttons.

"That's a great idea," Aubrey said. "Mom, can we play our song now?"

"I don't see why not," she said, reaching for her autoharp. "But Tenney, are you sure you're up for the jam today? You've had quite the adventure the past few days."

My fingers were callused and sore from playing my guitar every day, and I was more exhausted than I had ever been. But nothing could stop me from enjoying my favorite Christmas tradition with my family—not even a snowstorm.

"It wouldn't be Christmas without a family jam," I said. "Besides, I have a new song to play for all of you."

"We can't wait to hear it," Mom said. "Ready, Aubrey?"

As I listened to Mom and Aubrey play their song, I thought I might burst with joy. I had never been so happy to be home.

ABOUT THE AUTHOR

As a young reader, Kellen Hertz loved L. Frank Baum's Wizard of Oz series. But since the job of Princess of Oz was already taken, she decided to become an author. Alas, her unfinished first novel was lost in a sea of library books on the floor of her room, forcing her to seek other employment. Since then Kellen has worked as a screenwriter, television producer, bookseller, and congressional staffer. She made her triumphant return to novel writing when she coauthored *Lea and Camila* with Lisa Yee before diving into the Tenney series for American Girl. Kellen lives with her husband and their son in Los Angeles.

READY FOR AN ENCORE?

VISIT

americangirl.com

for Tenney's world

OF BOOKS, **APPS,**

GAMES, **QUIZZES,**

activities,

AND MORE!

Parents, request a FREE catalogue at
americangirl.com/catalogue

Sign up at americangirl.com/email
to receive the latest news and exclusive offers

Meet
Gabriela
McBride

American Girl®
Gabriela
by Teresa E. Harris

When the city threatens to close her beloved community arts center, Gabriela is determined to find a way to help. Can she harness the power of her words and rally her community to save Liberty Arts?

American Girl®
The Real Z
by Jen Calonita

Meet
Z Yang™

Z Yang is an expert at making stop motion movies, but now she has to make a documentary. Where to start?! And will her ideas be good enough for a real film festival?

✪ American Girl®
⚑ SCHOLASTIC

A group of girls so close, they're just

Like Sisters

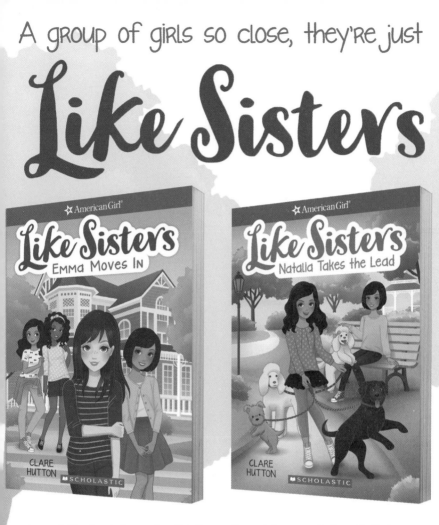

Emma loves visiting her twin cousins, Natalia and Zoe, so she's thrilled when her family moves to their town after living 3,000 miles away. Emma knows her life is about to change in a big way. And it will be more wonderful and challenging than any of the girls expect!

Several dogs are staying with their owners at the family's B&B. Natalia eagerly volunteers to watch and walk all of them with the help of her sister Zoe and her cousin Emma. But Zoe and Emma have their own commitments, and Natalia is quickly overwhelmed. When one of the dogs goes missing, will Natalia be able to step up and make things right?